POISONS & PAGES

A LIBRARY WITCH MYSTERY

ELLE ADAMS

My best friend was stuck in an enchanted sleep, and it was all my fault.

I turned the pages of the journal fervently, as though I might find a solution to all my problems nestled within its covers.

My crow familiar, Jet, supervised from his perch on my shoulder. "Any luck, partner?" he asked for about the fiftieth time.

"Nope." I'd made a habit of skimming through the book during breaks between visitors to the library, but translating the made-up code in which my dad had written the journal was somewhat difficult with an excitable crow bouncing around. "Do you want to go and help Estelle with the Halloween event planning?"

"She said she needed to make some calls alone, partner!"

"Ah."

Making phone calls would also be tricky with a talkative crow in the background, but I kind of wished my familiar would get a new hobby. Since my Aunt Candace had taken to spending every moment of her spare time trying to get into a secret room inside the equally secret, newly rediscovered fourth-floor corridor, she often forgot to ask Jet to bring her the latest gossip from the rest of town.

I couldn't believe that over a month had passed since Aunt Candace cracked the code for the corridor's secret door, but she still hadn't managed to get inside. But my best friend, Laney, had fallen into a coma around that time, and I was still no closer to figuring out a solution. Living in a magical library with pretty much every book in existence should've helped point me in the right direction, but the library itself was a creation of my late grandmother, and she'd left us to uncover its secrets without a map—in a literal sense and a metaphorical one.

Jet bounced across the desk like a feathery ping-pong ball. "Do you want me to put the returns away?"

"No… leave it to me."

Jet was scarcely bigger than my hand, but that didn't deter him from trying to lift huge textbooks and accidentally dropping them on the floor instead.

"Or maybe ask Spark to help," I said. "Is he around?"

I assumed Estelle didn't want the excitable pixie butting in on her phone calls, either, but I hadn't seen Spark all day.

"I think he's with your Aunt Candace, partner."

I groaned. "He isn't, is he?"

"I saw them go upstairs together." He fluttered anxiously. "Should I fetch him?"

"Sure—go ahead."

He took off, while I opened the journal once again and tried to find the spot where I'd left off. Finding any answers in it was a long shot, I knew, but the journal had belonged to my dad, who'd been intertwined with the magical world far before I became aware of its existence myself. Working through the complex code in which my dad had written the entries had been a months-long endeavour, and I still had a long way to go before I reached the end, but I lived in the hope that he might have dropped a clue that would get me out of my current dilemma.

Now that summer and the back-to-school season were over with, the comparative lack of visitors to the library should've meant that I would have a bit more time, but certain family members of mine rarely got through the day without unleashing some disaster or other.

Soon enough, Aunt Candace sauntered over to the desk. "Did you send your familiar to badger me?"

"Only to make sure you didn't turn Spark into a pencil."

Lean and willowy with wild, curly red hair, my aunt always looked as if she'd been interrupted in the middle of writing, which was usually true. Her mismatched flower-patterned skirt and blouse were bright enough that spotting the glittery purple pixie perched on her shoulder took me a moment.

"Now, why would I do that?" She wagged a finger at me. "I only borrowed him for this morning."

"Estelle won't like that."

"Estelle is too busy to notice." Her mouth tilted upward in amusement. "It's nearly Halloween already, is it?"

"Yep." We'd fallen behind on decorating, and while pumpkins certainly wouldn't look out of place amid the library's towering stacks and hidden corners, I wasn't in a particularly celebratory mood.

"Don't look so morose," Aunt Candace said. "Unless you're practising to be a zombie for the party. Then that expression on your face is perfect."

I made a noncommittal noise. If not for my desire to support my cousin, I'd kind of hoped to spend the night reading a book instead of going to the party myself. But leaving Estelle in charge of wrangling the guests wouldn't be fair—not to mention Aunt Candace, who would no doubt unleash her own personal brand of chaos at the party.

"Or a Reaper," she added with a snort of laughter. "I'd like to see the look on that Grim Reaper's face if we all dress up as him. I wonder if the fancy dress shop has any scythes?"

"Please don't."

The Grim Reaper had quite enough reasons to be annoyed at me without adding impersonation to the list.

"Nor the vampires, either, before you make that suggestion," I added.

Aunt Candace tipped her head to one side. "Are any of the vampires planning to attend the party?"

"I hope not." Evangeline and her fellow vampires were decidedly on the wrong side of creepy, and they didn't need to attend our parties when they held their own at the renovated old church that they'd made their home.

"I think you should invite them." She grinned. "It'd be a riot."

"Or a bloodbath." I rubbed my temples. "Have you had any luck upstairs?"

"No, and don't change the subject."

"I'm not," I replied, indicating the little pixie perched on her shoulder. "I want to know what you were doing with Spark."

"Nothing." A shrug. "I wondered if a nonhuman might be able to get through the door."

I frowned. "What would give you that idea?"

"The riddle asked for my heart's desire, but I contain far too many desires to be simplified in a single request." She spoke with a dramatic flourish. "A simpler creature has simpler desires."

"That's not very kind of you." I didn't know how much English the pixie understood, but he didn't seem bothered by her comment. "Simple or not, he's not your guinea pig."

Furthermore, a pixie was unlikely to succeed at getting through the door that had stumped my entire family. My aunt had needed a powerful translator spell to crack the code written on the door in the first place. The Spell Assistant, like the corridor itself, was one of Grandma's own creations, but it had been stolen from the library years before and had found its way back into our hands only when one of the Founders' would-be human recruits stole from them in turn. Yet even the Spell Assistant couldn't help us figure out the actual meaning of the riddle.

Speak your heart's desire. We'd all tried, addressing the door with everything from petty requests to deeply buried ambitions—but none had worked. Aunt Candace alone persisted, while the rest of us had gone back to our everyday routines without expending too much energy on the corridor and its mysterious magic.

"Don't be such a worrywart," my aunt added. "You should be going out, having fun, not moping over a desk."

"I've never been a party animal. And someone has to watch the front door for visitors."

My Aunt Adelaide was upstairs in the alchemy division, Estelle was occupied with planning the Halloween event, and Cass—I didn't know what Cass was doing, except that it probably involved dangerous magical creatures.

"Anyway, I'd have thought you'd want to help Aunt Adelaide hunt down details of rare poisons. Isn't that more of a worthwhile exercise than poking a door that doesn't want to open?"

"You would say that," she said. "You have a vested interest in the subject."

"Can you blame me?" Given her usual interest in anything weird or dangerous, I'd hoped her own interests would line up with Aunt Adelaide's quest to research vampire-killing poisons, but apparently not. "I'd have thought you'd be first in line to try out the recipe."

Under normal circumstances, handing my aunt Candace the means of brewing a deadly poison was a recipe for disaster, pun intended, but this particular brew was complex enough that she'd soon lost interest in figuring out the ingredients and had gone back up to the fourth floor instead—no matter that a poison that could stop a vampire's heart would have also been useful in our ongoing struggle against the Founders. She'd replied that she was a writer and not an alchemist, and that was that.

"Ask the vampires instead," she said. "When *did* you last speak to Evangeline?"

"Last week, and I don't want to bother her." I was constantly struggling not to check up on Evangeline's own research into possible cures for the poison more frequently, but pestering a centuries-old vampire was a spectacular way to end up locked in a coffin.

Aunt Candace scoffed. "I bet she has all the answers hidden inside that pretty head of hers. Vampires are hoarders of knowledge."

"If she knew of a cure, she wouldn't have kept it from me." *I hope.* The poison that had put Laney to sleep was rare enough that the sole recipe in existence was only available as an untranslated scribble on an ancient piece of parchment, which suggested that any existing cure was likely to be equally hard to access, even for a vampire as ancient and knowledgeable as Evangeline.

Despite her dire state, Laney had been incredibly lucky. At a higher dose, the poison was capable of stopping even a vampire's undead heart. Yet that didn't stop my sense of guilt from her ingesting the poison while preventing one of the Founders' vampires from clawing my face off. The others had told me over and over not to blame myself, but the fact was that she'd been in that situation only because of me.

"If Evangeline doesn't know, one of her other fanged friends will." A wicked smile curved her mouth. "Just give me the word, and I'll offer her an invitation to the party. It won't be that hard to spike her drink with truth potion."

"Aunt Candace." Horror washed over me. "Evangeline can read minds. She won't be fooled by a simple ruse. Also, I'm not sure truth potions even work on vampires."

"Some do." She burst out laughing. "Your *face*, Rory. The idea of going and asking her in person doesn't seem that bad now, does it?"

"You were trying to goad me into paying the vampires a visit?" *It'd almost worked too. Except...* "Can truth potions work on vampires? I mean, if there's a poison that can affect them, they aren't immune to all potions."

"No." A thoughtful expression came over her. "I wonder if those alchemical tomes might tell me more."

"That's right, go and help Aunt Adelaide." I wasn't sure my other aunt would appreciate her assistance, but that would be an improvement on her skulking around the fourth-floor corridor and using Estelle's pixie sidekick as an unwitting target on which to test her theories on how to open the sealed door.

"If I brew one of those potions, we'll need a lab rat," she said as though she'd picked up on my line of thought.

My shoulders tensed. "What, Laney?"

"No, of course not." Aunt Candace jabbed a finger at the carpeted floor. "Our sleepy friend in the basement."

"He's been asleep for decades."

That was possibly a result of the very same poison, but he certainly hadn't consented to her testing more potions on him. My aunts didn't even know the sleeping vampire's name, though he was known among our family as Albert. "Have you ever tried to wake him up before?"

"Of course. I've used every spell and potion that I know of, but without any luck." A sigh passed her lips. "I spent many weeks down there as a youth. I hoped that we might have a passionate affair when he awakened, but it was not to be."

I rolled my eyes. "I'm sure Albert will be thrilled to learn you've been ogling him when he eventually wakes up. Do you think he *was* affected by the same poison as Laney?"

The Founders normally gave the poison to their recruits with instructions to use it on themselves if they were captured by the enemy, but the vampire in the basement had been there since my grandmother's day. I wondered if she'd been the one who'd poisoned him or someone else. I was only guessing that he'd been a recipient of the same poison at all, but very few methods exist for incapacitating a vampire, much less putting one to sleep for decades or longer.

"I haven't the faintest idea," Aunt Candace said. "If my mother went to the trouble of obtaining the ingredients to brew a poison that rare, you'd think she'd have left us a sample, but I haven't found one."

"You didn't ask the sealed door for that... did you?" *Of course she did.*

While that would admittedly be a simpler option than brewing the poison ourselves, nothing in our lives was ever as simple as it seemed, even a door that cryptically declared it could grant our heart's desires.

"If you want the poison that badly, why not follow the recipe yourself?" she asked. "I see the merits of loading up a water gun with the poison and taking aim at the Founders from a safe distance."

"If the ingredients are as rare as you say, it won't be that easy." I'd been studying magic for less than a year, and advanced potions were far beyond my current level. "More people would have discovered the poison if it'd been easy to brew. I wonder why the Founders created a poison capable of killing their fellow vampires at all."

"To deal with anyone who might give away their secrets, I would guess," Aunt Candace said. "I can think of a thousand possible reasons. Some of them are going into my next book."

"Please don't get killed by the Founders for putting their secrets in writing."

"It's *fiction*, Rory. You can write anything, and nobody will believe it." And on that note, she skipped away, the pixie still riding her shoulder.

"Honestly." I shook my head. "Well, I can hardly tick off the Founders more than I already have."

Since I'd moved into the library the past winter, I'd encountered the group of knowledge-seeking vampires more times than I'd wanted to, and once had been bad enough. First, they tried to steal my dad's journal and got me fired from my former job at my dad's old bookshop in the process. My family members swooped in to rescue me from the Founders' pursuit and swept me away into their magical library, but the vampires had been a recurring blot on my time in the magical world.

"Partner?" Jet hopped onto my shoulder again. "Should I follow her?"

"Go ahead," I told my familiar. "Make sure she doesn't bother Aunt Adelaide too much, okay?"

As he launched into flight, I returned my attention to the journal. Thanks to the slow translation process, I was currently mired in the middle of a series of entries on my dad's attempts to find an old book of spells, a rare first edition of some kind. He'd had an uncanny knack for fixating on books that were also wanted by the vampiric collectors of rare tomes, but in fairness, the Founders seemed to want *every* rare book, whether its subject matter concerned the vampires or not.

That included the journal itself, which had been written in code both to keep the Founders at bay and to keep from exposing the magical world to me or to my mother. My mum had been a normal, and there were strict rules against bringing nonmagical people into this world. As a result, I'd grown up on the outside. Knowing I'd been a toddler when these diary entries were being written didn't stop the faint pang of regret that stirred when I read any mention of my family members in the journal.

I spoke to my sisters, and they mentioned one of Mother's inventions went missing recently, I read. *I have to admit I forgot it was still in the library. It'll come in handy if anyone ever needs to read this.*

I wondered if he was talking about the Spell Assistant. A note was scribbled in the margins, added to a later date, and I hastened to turn the page sideways to properly read the words.

It never did show up, Dad's note read. *Strange. Adelaide thinks Candace broke it and won't admit to anything, but I have a hard time believing any creation of Mother's could be easily broken. She always understood that the most powerful spells are those which concern the magic of possibility...*

Sylvester came swooping down to land behind me and cut off my concentration. "Why the long face?"

"Sylvester, do you remember when the Spell Assistant went missing?" I asked the owl.

"What kind of question is that? I know everything."

"You do remember." I jabbed a finger at the page. "According to this, my aunts thought the Spell Assistant had been left in a spare room and didn't realize it was missing for years. Did you look for it at all?"

"That's not my job," he said petulantly. "I can't be expected to keep track of every corner of this place."

"You *are* this place. Technically speaking." I spoke in a low voice, though nobody was close enough to overhear.

In response, Sylvester let out a screech that made my ears throb with pain.

"What is going on?" Aunt Adelaide came walking over, looking mildly frazzled. "Your Aunt Candace has decided to remove half the books in the alchemy section. I was going to consult those."

"Sorry, that's my fault," I said. "I was trying to distract her from using poor Spark the pixie to test out new ideas on how to get through that door."

"Oh, your aunt hardly needs an excuse to cause mischief." She tutted. "Sylvester, can you help me carry these books upstairs?"

"Certainly not," he said. "I don't have hands."

"You have feet, and you're just being awkward."

The owl made a rude noise. "Everyone is so argumentative today. I went to see the vampire girl, and you would've thought I'd put a dead mouse in her bed from the way *certain* people reacted."

My attention snapped over to him. "You visited Laney?"

"I thought that if I recited poetry, it might wake her up."

I didn't know whether to laugh or scold him. "Wait, who argued with you? Laney is..." *Asleep.* That meant someone else was in her room.

Aunt Adelaide stepped in. "I can take over the desk, Rory, if you want to check up on her."

From her tone, I didn't know whether she meant Laney or Cass. My other cousin had taken to watching over Laney voluntarily for reasons I hadn't figured out. I hadn't realised Cass was up there today and not on the third floor with her animals. I didn't think she would be any more pleased to see me than she'd been to see Sylvester, but at least I had no intention of reciting poetry at either of them.

"Thanks." I left my aunt arguing with the owl and crossed the lobby to the corridor that led to our family's living quarters.

From there, I climbed the winding staircase to the first floor, where my room and Estelle's were located as well as the guest room that Laney had claimed as her own. I slowed my pace when I reached the room, whose door lay partly open.

Taking a deep breath, I entered. When Cass rose upright from her seat beside Laney's bed, I froze, unable to look directly at my best friend's still body. Since vampires didn't need to breathe, she might as well have been a corpse.

"Sorry." I stumbled back into the doorway. "Didn't mean to interrupt. Sylvester mentioned he was in here tormenting you…"

"Relax." Cass turned back to Laney. "I'm not going to bite your head off. I already did that to the owl."

"I figured," I said. "I don't know if he thought he was helping or just trying to be annoying."

"More like he was irritated at me for asking the Book of Questions to give us an antidote."

I raised an eyebrow. "How many times have you asked now?"

"I've tried at least a dozen versions of the same question," she replied. "He said the library doesn't contain that information. That doesn't mean one doesn't exist."

"Right…" My gaze caught on the book half open on Cass's lap, but she pointedly put it aside before I could glimpse the title. "How is she?"

"There's no change," she told me. "Unless Aunt Candace has decided to start experimenting with cures?"

"No… Well, she's up in the alchemy section, but she's

more interested in figuring out which other potions work on vampires. Like truth potions."

Her brow arched. "I hope she doesn't plan on testing them on anyone."

"Except for the vampire in the basement, no." I drew in a breath. "She also suggested that Evangeline isn't being entirely honest with us about her own knowledge on the subject."

Cass snorted. "Obviously. Evangeline's a centuries-old vampire. Deceit is hardwired into her."

"I guess." My throat closed up when I caught sight of Laney's expressionless face out of the corner of my eye. Any hopes of curing her rested amongst her fellow undead, and only one place had the slightest chance of providing that knowledge.

"Go on," she said. "One of us has to go and ask more questions, and you're more diplomatic than I am."

"Diplomatic?" I echoed. "Is that the most important trait I need to deal with Evangeline?"

"Better than Aunt Candace's approach."

"True."

Aunt Candace had nearly landed herself in trouble by interrogating the vampires in a much less subtle manner than I was capable of. "I'll see what the others say."

I forced myself to take one last look at Laney before I left the room. Cass was far stronger than I was, to spend so much time in here without breaking down, but she at least hadn't been responsible for Laney's current state. She also didn't blame me for it, for a wonder.

When I walked downstairs, Estelle was waiting for me in the living room. "No change?"

"No." I buried my hands in my pockets. "No, and I think we're only going to get anywhere if we're willing to look outside of the library. It's been a while since I last spoke to Evangeline and asked for an update."

Estelle blanched. "Only because she actually *would* bite your head off if you asked too many questions."

"She's the one with the contacts, though."

Even my dad hadn't been on friendly terms with the Founders—and for all Evangeline's claims that she wasn't one of them, she'd lived for hundreds of years and had been acquainted with the other vampires even since long before my grandmother's day.

"I don't know. It was just an idea," I said. "How's the Halloween planning going?"

"I'm taking a break. Still no visitors?"

"Nope." I walked with her to the desk, where her mother sat thumbing through the record book.

Sylvester had vanished, probably to sulk, unless she'd managed to convince him to carry the books upstairs after all. "Hey, Aunt Adelaide… do you think I should pay Evangeline another visit? Aunt Candace suggested she was withholding information on curing Laney."

"I wouldn't advise you to take my sister up on any of her suggestions, Rory."

"No, but… well, I haven't spoken to them for a while," I said. "Evangeline doesn't seem to pay visits to the library anymore either."

Ancient vampires showing up on the doorstep and hovering around looking creepy wasn't necessarily good for business, but it probably said something about her level of faith in our own progress that she hadn't come to ask us whether we'd had any breakthroughs of our own.

Estelle glanced at her mother. "If you want to go, I'll come with you. Jet too."

Aunt Adelaide exhaled in a sigh. "If you're sure, but please be careful."

2

Estelle and I left the library and crossed the town square to the high street. The day was overcast and chilly, hardly the weather to visit a beach town, which would explain the lack of tourists. Granted, people came to see the library all year round, and its presence was a constant impressive landmark, five storeys of towering brick overlooking the square.

Equally impressive was the manor house in which the vampires made their home, though considerably different in atmosphere. Renovated from an old church, the house towered over its neighbours, and while it wasn't dark yet, all the grey clouds in the sky seemed to cluster around the rooftops.

Trepidation gripped me as I knocked on the wooden door, and several tense minutes passed before it opened, revealing a female vampire with a dramatic sweep of dark hair.

"Is Evangeline in?" I asked the vampire.

The vampire bared her teeth in response. "Aurora, is it? She expected you to show up some time ago."

"Huh?" *She expected me? Really?*

The new vampire vanished, and when Evangeline appeared in her place, I instantly forgot what I was intending to say. Evangeline had that effect. Like most vampires, she possessed a kind of ethereal beauty that went far beyond her glossy hair and nearly glowing pale face. The prey instinct in my lizard brain told me I was being chased by a lion, utterly blanking out all other thoughts.

"Speak, Aurora," Evangeline said.

"I was wondering if you had any updates on... on your search for the Founders." I tripped over the words, trying to steer clear of any subjects that might incite a bad reaction. The last Founder I'd interacted with, Cateline, had died in custody, choosing to poison herself rather than spill her secrets to Evangeline. That was still a sore point with the vampires' leader, and I didn't need to get the door slammed in my face after having spent so long working up the nerve to come.

"No," she said. "I don't."

That... was considerably less detailed than I hoped for. "Then why did you expect me to visit?"

"You're human, Aurora, and woefully predictable."

My heart sank, but I stood my ground. "Human or not, I'm willing to help find the Founders myself if there's anything I can do.

"Now, would your family members want you risking your life?" She eyed Estelle, who shrank away from her stare. "I don't think so. Besides, you've caused too much of a stir to infiltrate the Founders' ranks without being detected."

"Infiltrate?" I echoed. "Is that your plan? Send in spies?"

"Why not?" she asked. "The Founders have proven quite impossible to track following recent events. I suspect that to find their current location, a stealthier approach will be necessary."

"Which Founders did you mean?"

Mortimer Vale and his two close companions were in jail, while Carlos Verdant and his own allies had either run away following the fire at the vampires' house or had met a grisly end at Evangeline's hands.

Besides, who could possibly get away with infiltrating the Founders' ranks without being caught? Not me, that's for sure. I would walk through fire to save Laney, but I would get caught in a heartbeat if any Founders were present who might be passingly familiar with the ones whom I'd made enemies of. Yet I had a hard time believing Evangeline had learned *nothing* over the course of the past few weeks.

Evangeline laughed, a musical sound. "You're certainly bolder than you were when we first met, Aurora, but I'm afraid I'm going to have to disappoint you. I haven't managed to convince any of my own allies to infiltrate the Founders' ranks."

True, no doubt, but that couldn't be her only idea. Right?

"Please," I found myself saying. "Please, if there's anything you know, tell me."

It'd been weeks since Laney had fallen into her coma, and I'd made zero progress toward finding a way to free her from her current state. The library, for once, had failed me. Like it or not, Evangeline was the one person I knew of with the connections and skills that could help me save my best friend, and for that reason, I was willing to persist with my questioning, far past the point where any sensible person would have stopped before they found themselves locked in the dungeon.

Evangeline spoke. "If you insist, Aurora, I have heard rumours that the fire did not entirely destroy Ridgeway House. It's possible that some of their possessions survived."

"The Founders aren't using that building any longer, are they?"

"No," she said. "The fire damage was extensive enough that none have dared to return, but I've glimpsed some rather interesting rumours in the thoughts of people who've passed by the house recently. While I have found nothing on the property myself, you might have more luck, Aurora. That is all the information I have."

"Thank you," I said carefully. "I appreciate the tip."

She withdrew into the house while I wondered if these rumours were merely a ruse designed to get me to go away. It was in Evangeline's interests to find an antidote for the poison as well, but being immortal, vampires didn't lack for patience, and Evangeline probably hadn't even noticed how much time had passed since Laney had fallen into a coma—not long enough to take urgent action.

"I don't think taking her advice is a good idea," Estelle whispered to me as we made our way back to the library. "Why would she want you to go back to the Founders' house?"

"I don't know," I replied. "She might be trying to placate me. I mean, it's unlikely I'll find anything in there that her people haven't already stumbled upon."

The place had been on fire, which was kind of off-putting to most vampires, but the flames had had a long time to burn themselves out.

"That's true, but I still don't think it's a good idea to set foot in their house again."

"You aren't wrong." I pulled up the hood of my cloak when drizzle began to mist the air around us. "I wish I'd asked for more details about these supposed rumours she heard in people's thoughts."

When we reached the library, Estelle wasted no time in telling her mother what Evangeline had imparted to us, and I was unsurprised when Aunt Adelaide put her foot down. "I wouldn't go, Rory."

"I know," I said. "It's not much of a clue, but we haven't seen the Founders in weeks."

Evangeline had worked hard to keep them out of the area, but how was I supposed to wake Laney from her coma without an antidote? The Founders were the only people who might have a cure—not that they knew I needed one. Laney hadn't been the intended target of the poison, and if the Founders caught on, there was nothing to stop them from leveraging my desperation against me and against my family. At least searching their empty house wouldn't guarantee an encounter with the vampires themselves, though I knew better than to expect to find a cure hidden in a cupboard.

A knock on the library door made me spin around, though I relaxed a moment later. The only person polite enough to knock even when the library was open to the public was my boyfriend, Xavier.

I opened the door to reveal the one person who could lift my spirits without fail—no pun intended, though he *was* the Grim Reaper's apprentice, not that anyone would know by looking at his angelic blond hair and bright aquamarine eyes. The scythe strapped to his back was the only clue—that and his all-black attire, which meant he would fit right in at a Halloween party without the need for a fancy-dress costume.

"Hey, Rory," he said. "I saw you leaving Evangeline's house. Everything okay?"

"Yeah." I greeted him with a hug. "I asked her if she'd found any more clues about how to save Laney, and she mentioned there was a chance we might find something at the Founders' old hideout."

"You know she's not exactly the most trustworthy individual."

"She's not out to get me killed," I replied. "I don't know that there *is* anything there, but the house is the only place in the area that the Founders had permanent lodgings at. That we know of, anyway."

"They won't have left anything behind," he said. "If they did, Evangeline would have taken it."

"I know." I chewed on my lower lip. "It's driving me mad, though, not having so much as a smidgen of information. Would you come with me? Just for peace of mind?"

Xavier took my hand. "Of course I'll go with you. Just give me a minute to confirm with my boss."

———

The universe—or, rather, the Grim Reaper—had other ideas. While my family members grudgingly agreed to let me go to the Founders' old house as long as I stayed close to Xavier, I received an unwelcome message as the library was closing that evening, saying that the Grim Reaper had called him out on an urgent mission and that he had no idea when he'd be back.

What's so urgent? I pocketed my phone, wishing some of the other members of my family were around. Aunt Adelaide had gone to stop her sister from upending the alchemy division, while Estelle was back to working on Halloween preparations.

"What is it, partner?" Jet squeaked, having reappeared near the desk at closing time.

"I wanted to look around the Founders' old hideout with Xavier," I admitted. "But none of the others are downstairs. Can you find Aunt Candace?"

Cass wouldn't want to be dragged out on an errand in the rain, but Aunt Candace never passed up an opportunity for book research. I didn't expect anything to come of our visit to the house, but if there weren't any vampires present, she shouldn't be able to drag us both into trouble. In theory.

I busied myself tidying the Reading Corner until Jet came swooping down from the balcony. "She's turned herself into a wall, partner!"

"You mean Aunt Candace?" *A wall?* That was a new one.

"Yes, and your aunt and cousin are trying to turn her back."

I groaned. "How did she manage that? Is she in the alchemy division?"

"No, the fourth-floor corridor!"

Oh no. Evidently, she hadn't learned her lesson from the time she'd accidentally wiped her own memory. *Why, Aunt Candace?* My own magical skills were slightly below average, and nothing about that corridor was remotely typical of the paranormal world. "Not sure I can be much help with that."

"I'll go to the house with you, partner!" said Jet.

"Erm…" I trailed off, not wanting to hurt his feelings. To be fair, he could be helpful, but he was also a chatterbox whose idea of stealth was dropping a book on my head. "It'll be dark soon."

"Not yet." Jet let out a chirp. "I know where the house is. I'll go, partner."

"Wait." My heart sank when he flapped his little wings and zoomed off. "Hang on. I need to tell the others."

"I'll go, partner!" His squeak rang across the lobby, and in moments, he'd vanished through the open window.

"Jet, I didn't mean now," I said ineffectually. *Dammit, Aunt Candace.* I'd known my familiar was desperate to make himself useful, but I hadn't expected him to be *that* keen to visit the vampires' abandoned house. "Sylvester, where are you?"

No response came from the owl. No doubt, he was upstairs laughing at Aunt Candace's predicament, but a rush of frustration and resolve overtook me in equal measures. *All right, then.*

I opened the front door, but my familiar had long since vanished over the rooftops. Pulling my hood up to keep the rain off my face, I retrieved my wand from my pocket.

My mental image of Ridgeway House remained vivid enough for me to use a transportation spell, and while I knew my family wouldn't be thrilled at my choice, I dreaded to think what kind of trouble Jet might get into by himself.

Here we go. I pictured the grand house and waved my wand. Between one blink and the next, Ivory Beach disappeared, and my feet touched down on the gravel path leading from the country lane to the fancy estate the Founders had once made their home—or some of the Founders had. The building was a gutted ruin, and while I'd set it ablaze myself, a quiver of surprise arose at how effectively the fire had eaten through the insides of the building. The bricks were intact, but the windows had all blown out, and the stench of burning lingered around the property.

Jet descended and landed on my arm. "I don't see anyone in there, partner!"

"Best be quiet," I whispered. "Listen—can you fly through the upstairs window and have a look around? Try not to be seen."

"Sure!" He spiralled upward toward the open window and vanished inside.

I waited outside for a long, tense moment until he returned.

"Nobody's in the house, partner, but I don't like it. It's creepy."

All right. "You should wait outside. I won't be long."

The wooden door hung off its hinges, and I nudged it open as carefully as I could manage. Then I entered, a shiver trailing down my spine as I passed the open door to the once-grand ballroom where the vampires had danced with their human subjects.

The smell of burning permeated the air, making my eyes water, and the chill intensified at the memory of being drawn into the vampires' midst. *Wait...* It was more than the cold that made me feel as if I was stepping on someone's grave. I knew that sensation.

A figure flickered into view, and my steps came to a halt as I made out a young woman hovering above the burned floorboards. Literally hovering. *A ghost. I knew it.*

When she saw me watching her, she gasped. "I thought there was nobody else in here."

Does she know she's dead? I trod closer, heart in my mouth. "Who are you?"

"Bailey." She stared at me, her eyes round and terrified. "Help me, please. I'm… I'm looking for my friend."

My heart sank. If she and her friend had been present at one of the Founders' gatherings, it didn't take a genius to figure out how she'd met her end… but was the same true of the person she was looking for?

"Partner?" Jet flew into the room and then withdrew, beating his little wings. "It's so cold in here!"

He couldn't see the ghost, but animals had an uncanny ability to sense things that humans couldn't. The ghost recoiled at Jet's cry, shrinking into a corner.

"I'm okay, Jet," I called to my familiar. "Wait for me outside."

I'd thought ghosts showed up only immediately after they'd died, but this poor soul might have been wandering the deserted corridors for weeks. I couldn't imagine she'd have wanted to talk to any vampires who might come into the house, even ones who weren't Founders. Was this why Evangeline had sent me here instead?

"Who's your friend?" I asked her quietly. "Maybe I can help."

Footsteps sounded in the hall. *Living* footsteps. The ghost jumped violently enough that she hovered several feet off the ground, then she rose upward through the ceiling and vanished into the room above.

Oh no. My body tensed as the footsteps halted outside the door. Heart in my mouth, I pulled out my wand and walked across the ballroom. It wasn't a vampire—they were too stealthy to make a sound if they didn't want to—but when I ducked into the hallway, I didn't see anyone else there.

"Boo," Cass said.

I jumped, hand to my chest. "*Cass.* Did you follow me here?"

"What do you think?" She tutted. "You should have asked me to come with you."

"I didn't think…"

"Didn't think I'd be interested?" Her eyes glittered with amusement. "Wrong."

"I was going to say I didn't think I'd actually find anything here." I pointed upward at the ceiling. "But I did, and now she's run off."

"If she's a ghost, she's tied to this building," Cass said. "We can find her again."

"Not necessarily. She's terrified."

Ghosts were capable of hiding themselves if they didn't want to be found, and from what I'd heard, it didn't take too much of a shock to cause them to dive into the deeper after-world, never to return.

"I bet she's more scared of the vampires than us," Cass said. "We can find her."

"All right." I walked down the corridor toward the stairs, gladder than I would admit that she'd shown up to keep me company. The scent of burning was even stronger on the floor above, which made sense because the fire had started on the upper level. I didn't regret what I'd done, but the ghost… when had she died? The image of the flames eating through the curtains was still fresh in my mind, and part of me half expected to find a furious vampire lurking on the landing and waiting to dispense justice against us for destroying their home.

Cass grabbed my arm and jabbed a finger at a closed door, mouthing, "In there."

I swivelled toward the door and heard a faint whisper from behind it. Two people were speaking, and neither sounded like the ghost.

"Be *quiet*," a feminine voice hissed. "I swear I saw the ghost over there, but if you're going to make a lot of unnecessary noise—"

"Spoilsport," a second voice returned, more masculine and considerably louder. "I don't make unnecessary noise. Everything I do is very necessary."

Who are they? I didn't know how I hadn't heard them enter the house.

Cass strode ahead of me and shoved the door open, raising her wand. "Nobody move."

The two strangers, who'd been standing beside the window, swivelled toward us. One of them *was* a ghost, a man with short curly hair and a wide grin. His female companion—scowling and pale, with dark hair that looked as windswept as someone who'd just gotten off a broomstick— was very much alive.

"Who are you?" I asked. "What are you doing in here?"

"Looking for a ghost," the woman replied.

"Not that ghost, I assume?" I gestured at her companion, who gave a dramatic gasp.

"You can see me!" he exclaimed.

"I can, yes." Not every witch could, but my family members had that ability, and evidently, this woman did too. "Why are you looking for a ghost, exactly?"

"I'm a ghost blogger." She glared at her companion when

he snorted. "This is Mart, my brother. I'm Maura. Listen… you *did* see the ghost, didn't you?"

"You're lying," Cass said. "I think you're involved with the people who used to own this house."

"Who *did* own this house?" Mart asked. "There don't seem to be many personal belongings left behind."

"That's because it caught on fire," I said with a glance at my cousin. "Cass, I don't think they're with the Founders."

Cass grunted, unconvinced, but I doubted the Founders would recruit a random ghost and his witch sister. I was assuming she was a witch. She didn't give me shifter vibes and wasn't a vampire either, which left few options.

"Who?" Maura asked. "Founders… I've heard that name."

"How did you get in?" I asked. "We came through the door, and I didn't hear anyone upstairs."

Jet hadn't seen anyone either—nobody living, anyway, and the woman was no ghost.

Maura shrugged. "I used a transportation spell."

That would have made a noise. She did have a wand sticking out of her pocket, which backed up my witch theory, but something about her manner set me on edge all the same.

"I don't buy it," Cass said.

"Believe whatever you want." The woman stepped forward, her gaze on the open door behind me. "Listen, I really do need to find that ghost. So if you don't mind…"

Cass's hand shot out and caught Maura's arm. The second woman jumped back, her body blurring oddly. *That's familiar.*

"The shadows." I'd thought something was strange about the woman, and when she jumped out of Cass's way, her body grew shadowed in a way that suggested she was only half there. "You're a Reaper."

3

The woman tensed but didn't deny my accusation. Neither did her companion, whose smile had vanished and who was eyeing up the window as though contemplating a quick getaway.

"Another Reaper?" Cass queried. "Are you?"

Maura gave a sigh. "Fine. Yes, I am."

"Why is a Reaper wandering around this old house?" Cass asked. "Are you a rogue, I wonder?"

"A rogue?" I studied Maura's face. "Are you?"

"Easy enough question to answer," Cass said. "There's usually one Reaper assigned to a region, and you're dating this one's apprentice."

Thanks, Cass. My face heated as the two newcomers both stared openly at me.

"You're dating the Reaper?" Mart asked.

"His apprentice," I corrected. "And she has a point. This isn't your region. Why are you here, much less in a house that's been abandoned for months?"

"I really am a ghost blogger… Okay, my friend is, but I'm

helping her out," Maura said. "I have certain skills that make it easier to find ghosts than the average person."

"Like being an angel of death," Cass said.

Maura winced. "I'm half Reaper. Still mortal. Also, I'm not a rogue. More of a freelancer."

"Sounds like a rogue to me." Cass didn't budge from the doorway, nor did she lower her wand.

Mart's wary expression had given way to curiosity. "You're not dead," he remarked, drifting closer to me. "Why would you date a Reaper? Seems a waste of your life."

"None of your business," I said, taken aback by the personal comment.

"Mart, cut that out," Maura said. "You *are* dead. Make yourself useful, and help me find our elusive spirit."

He made a wounded noise. "You don't have to be so callous. I'm very sensitive."

"No, you aren't," his sister responded. "You were bragging about being the best-dressed dead person in the country earlier."

"We were looking for the ghost too," I said in an attempt to steer the conversation back on topic. "She spoke to me earlier, but she got spooked and ran off. Listen, do you know anything about the people who owned this house?"

"Nope," said Mart, whose cheery smile was back. "Haven't a clue. It's a bit gloomy, isn't it?"

They don't know. Cass remained distrustful, but my instincts told me that these two had stumbled in by complete accident. They might have secrets of their own, but Reapers were fundamentally opposed to vampires in general—most of the time. Surely, even a pair of misfit outsiders was no exception, whether they were rogues or not.

"The house," I said slowly, watching for Maura's reaction, "was owned by vampires."

"Really?" Surprise flickered in Maura's eyes. "Weird. They

don't tend to become ghosts when they die… not usually, anyway."

"It's not their ghost I'm looking for," I clarified. "She was human—"

"How'd they start a fire?" Mart interjected. "Sounds careless to me. No wonder they ran off in shame."

"Actually—" I broke off when Cass rammed an elbow into my side. "Ow. Cass, I told you. I don't think they're in league with the Founders."

Maura's brows shot up. "Founders? They're vampires?"

"Familiar with them, are you, Reaper?" Cass raised her wand again.

Maura heaved a sigh. "Please don't. I don't want to have to trap you in the afterworld. I don't think it's a productive use of my time or yours either."

Cass bared her teeth in a rather vampirelike manner. "Try me."

"Stop that." I stepped between them. "Cass, let her explain herself before you get both of us trapped inside the afterworld and I have to call Xavier to rescue us."

"Most people would run screaming in terror at the mere concept of being trapped on the other side," Maura remarked. "You're an interesting pair of witches, you are. Sisters?"

"Cousins," said Cass. "And don't change the subject."

"Where did you hear of the Founders?" I pressed on. "Also, who told you there was a ghost here?"

That was suspicious, but Reapers were attuned to ghosts in a way similar to Aunt Candace's knack for sniffing out a good story. It didn't necessarily mean anything was awry.

"In the neighbouring village," she said. "I heard some stories from the locals I spoke to who said there were often weird noises from the house at night. Apparently, it sounded like someone was throwing a party, but they also told me the house has been empty for weeks."

"The owners did used to throw parties," I said. "Before…"

"Before you burned down their house?" Maura guessed.

"Was I that obvious?" My face heated up. "It's not something I make a habit of doing."

"I gathered," said Maura. "You're full of surprises. Most vampires don't forgive minor slights, much less burning down their property."

"I already figured that one out myself," I said. "Met any vampires before?"

"Not really," she said. "I don't hang out with vampires, but I've heard the name 'Founders' mentioned once or twice. That's the extent of my knowledge. Sorry to disappoint you," she added to Cass.

"We have local vampires who'll be interested to ask you a few more questions," my cousin replied, undeterred. "You— what are you doing?"

Maura had made a sudden move for the hallway, only to find her way blocked by Cass again. "Move out of the way. Someone else is here."

"Are they?" I didn't hear anything downstairs, but Reapers were as attuned to the living as they were to the dead. "Where?"

Darkness appeared in the centre of the room, forming a shadowy figure holding a scythe. Mart gave a yell and hid behind his sister, Maura hissed out a breath, and even Cass took a step back into the doorway. My heart jumped into my throat, my pulse racing.

Then the shadows receded, revealing Xavier's face peering out from behind the scythe. "Rory?"

"Xavier." I stared at him in disbelief. "What are you doing here?"

"Looking for me, I guess," Maura put in. "Let me guess, you're the region's local Reaper?"

"That's right." He turned his attention to her ghostly companion for a moment then surveyed Maura herself. "Who exactly are you?"

"Maura," she replied. "A professional ghost blogger of sorts. I was looking for a local spirit, but I doubt it'll show itself with *two* Reapers in the house."

"Really." He turned to me next. "Was she already here when you came in?"

"I think she slipped in through the afterworld not long after I arrived," I guessed. "There *is* a ghost here, though, but she got freaked out and flew off. Otherwise, I think Maura's telling the truth."

Where *had* the ghost disappeared to? She might have thought Maura had come to banish her, which was a reasonable assumption, given what Reapers usually did to the dead. Add in Xavier joining us, and we'd be lucky if she hadn't dived straight through the doorway that led deeper into the afterworld.

"My boss sent me here," he said, "to catch a rogue Reaper. Be careful—she's not what she seems."

"I know she's a Reaper," I said. "I don't think she's a rogue, though."

"I'm not," Maura said. "I'm here to help a ghost, but I doubt she'll come back unless one or both of us leaves."

"Nice try," Cass put in. "I don't trust her. Xavier, you can Reap her soul, can't you?"

Maura paled. "There's no need for that. Besides, he probably can't swing that scythe without permission from his boss."

Xavier scowled at her. "I don't make a habit of removing people's souls without asking a few questions first. I'd like to know how you got here and why you're so far away from your own region."

"If you want to check with the Reaper Council, I've spoken to them before, and they can back me up," she said. "If you're less than keen on a trip all the way up north, I suppose you'll just have to take my word for it."

Cass scoffed. "Yeah, right."

Xavier shook his head. "I can't do that. Sorry."

"Look, I don't have a scythe, do I?" she said. "If I were a rogue, I'd have stolen one before I went on the run."

"Is that common?" I couldn't help asking. The Grim Reaper *had* had one of his scythes stolen once, on one memorable occasion, but I couldn't imagine they regularly turned their backs on the dangerous tools that made it possible to do their jobs.

"No," Xavier said. "But rogues aren't overly common, either, and these two showed up somewhere that we already have a reason to keep an eye on."

"Because of the vampires?" Maura asked. "Don't look at me like that. Your girlfriend told me herself. I wouldn't have known otherwise."

"I think she's right," I said. "There aren't any remnants of the Founders left in here. Nobody except for that ghost."

"One of their victims," Cass supplied. "I don't buy that a Reaper from another region is here by coincidence."

"If I wanted rid of the ghost, I don't need a scythe to banish her," Maura retaliated. "I could have pushed her into the afterworld and run off before you ever knew I was here. But I stuck around because I want answers."

"All right," Xavier said. "I'm inclined to give you the benefit of the doubt, but my boss might not be that forgiving. He's the one who sent me to find you, and it'll be easier if you come with me to set the record straight."

"Trust me, if I was a rogue, I'd be a lot more troublesome,"

Maura said. "I'm only here to find a ghost, nothing more, and I doubt she's coming back while we're in the same room. After we find her, we'll talk about meeting the boss."

Xavier didn't move, while Cass remained standing between the rest of us and the door. Maura locked eyes with her then with Xavier. "I don't suppose you'll let me use the afterworld to get out of this room?"

"No," said Xavier and Cass at the same time, in a bizarre moment of unity that had me wondering if I'd accidentally slipped into an alternate dimension.

"Then I guess we're at a stalemate." Maura folded her arms across her chest.

"Well, this is awkward," Mart commented. "Want me to drop things on their heads until one of them moves?"

Xavier's eyes narrowed. "Why do you have a ghost attached to you? He's not local."

"He's my brother," Maura said. "Also, the reason I left the Reapers."

"Really." Xavier looked between them, while Mart stuck his tongue out. "That's against the rules. Enough to make you a rogue, in fact."

"Most rogues *destroy* people's souls, not save them," Maura shot back at him. "I just want to be left alone. Both of us do."

"I don't," Mart supplied. "I want to be a celebrity."

"You came to a haunted house to avoid trouble?" Cass asked Maura, ignoring her ghostly brother. "Nope, I still don't believe you."

Xavier's mouth compressed. "I can't say my boss would like me to let you walk free. I'll have to report you to him regardless of your reasons for being here even if you don't come to him yourself."

"Feel free," Maura said. "I expect he already knows I'm here, and I'd rather not have him show up here too."

"Neither would I," said Mart. "Meanwhile, I say we stop standing around yapping and go and find our missing ghost."

"Agreed." Maura took a step forward then paused when Cass lifted her wand. "You can walk ahead of us if you like. I'm only trying to get out of this room. It smells horrible."

"Thanks to our pyromaniac here," Mart said, gesturing toward me.

"Don't be absurd." I ducked my head, flushing. "I only started a fire because we were running for our lives from a group of angry vampires. Anyway, both of you can walk through walls. You can find the ghost easily, can't you?"

"You'd be surprised." Maura moved forward again.

This time, Cass grudgingly let her walk past and stuck close behind her when she left the room. Mart drifted down the landing to join them, while I fell into step with Xavier.

"This was your mission?" I asked him.

Xavier nodded. "My boss detected a rogue Reaper and demanded I go after them at once. You know how he gets when he thinks someone is plotting against him."

"Yeah," I said. "Cass and I ran into those two when we were looking for a ghost. She was in the ballroom downstairs —the ghost, I mean—but Cass frightened her off."

"Ah." He dipped his head in understanding. "I'm glad you didn't come here alone."

Well... "Jet's here, too, but he got spooked and went to wait for me outside. Listen—the ghost was one of the Founders' victims, I'm sure. She was looking for her missing friend."

His expression darkened. "You think they were both at one of their gatherings?"

"Almost certainly," I murmured. "I don't know how long the ghost has been here, but it can't be much fun being trapped in the Founders' house."

"I can't sense any other spirits in here," Xavier said, "but they might have moved on."

"Might have." Ghosts didn't usually linger this long, but the dead could be surprisingly tenacious.

"She needs to be sent into the deeper afterworld," he added. "At a guess, this missing friend of hers constitutes unfinished business. That's the usual reason ghosts stay past their time. I can tell her I'll do my best to find out what happened to her friend and see if that's enough to convince her to move on."

"I think we need more information first," I whispered to him as we descended the stairs. "Who is she? And did anyone else die in the house? If the locals have been hearing loud noises, that points to there being more than one ghost. Unless Bailey's been talking to herself for weeks, which I somehow doubt."

"Evangeline told you that, did she?" He glanced at the back of Maura's head. "I think we need to keep the details of your own ties to the vampires quiet. Just in case."

Oh. I'd forgotten, momentarily, that Cateline had made an odd remark insinuating that some Reapers would take the Founders' side, given the chance. If Maura *had* known the Founders, we were running a major risk by letting her stick around while we spoke to the ghost again, but I had my doubts that she'd lied. For all we knew, she might be able to help us—and help the lost spirit too.

"I'll try, but they're the reason I'm here." I lowered my voice to keep Maura from overhearing, but she was too occupied with chasing her brother out of a broom cupboard to notice us whispering. "Also, I can't imagine the ghosts will reappear with two Reapers in the house. Not to mention a noisy ghost."

It didn't take long for our mismatched group to search all the downstairs rooms before returning to the ballroom. The large grand room brought another slew of unwelcome memories of that night my family and I had faced the Founders and narrowly escaped with our lives. *Was the ghost in here that night? When did she die?*

"This is where you first saw the ghost?" Maura scanned the dusty remnants of the once polished and shiny floor. "Who was she? Not a vampire."

"One of their victims, I think," I told her. "They used to bring humans here… normals. They'd drug them with vampire blood and then offer immortality."

Disgust flickered across her face. "Okay, that's vile. Let me guess, they weren't inclined to keep their promises after the biting part?"

"I assume not," I replied. "Unfortunately, they're fast, so most of the vampires were able to get away from the fire and fled the house before they got caught."

"And they left their poor victims behind?"

"I didn't see any bodies." A quiver of dread rose inside my chest. "Not that I had time to check every room."

Had there still been humans trapped in here? The thought made my stomach turn.

Seeing the look on my face, Xavier took my hand and squeezed. "There wasn't anyone in here. Not alive. Everyone got out."

How do you know? He hadn't been able to come and help us himself, and if there'd been any hidden rooms, I wouldn't have known. I'd been too occupied with ensuring my family escaped the vampires' clutches to consider that there might have been other victims trapped in here.

Maura glanced over at me. "How'd you end up in a vampire's house anyway?"

"They captured my family."

Cass shot me a warning look, but I didn't think I'd get anywhere by hiding the truth. Rogue or not, Maura wasn't bound to the orders of a more senior Reaper and therefore had nobody to tell tales to.

"Well, there's a quicker way to find a ghost." Maura raised a hand. "This ought to get her attention."

Shadows billowed outward and filled the room, and the afterworld answered her call.

4

Darkness filled the ballroom, masking the walls and windows, until the room vanished behind clouds thicker than smoke.

Xavier glared at Maura. "It's illegal to do that."

"Technically, it isn't," she said. "It's only illegal for me to summon or banish ghosts, and funnily enough, nobody complains when the things I banish are attacking the locals."

"What are you even doing?" I shivered, eyeing the darkness warily. "You don't need to call the afterworld here in order to summon a single ghost."

"No, but it'll stop you lot from distracting me." Maura lifted her head. "And it makes it easier for me to track the ghost's actual location. She can't hide from me in the afterworld."

"Unless she moves on," Xavier added. "Which is a risk."

"Maybe, but if she really has unfinished business, she'll want to stay." Maura pointed, and the shadows parted, revealing the open door at the side of the ballroom. "She's that way. One of you regular people should go ahead. She's more likely to talk to you than to a Reaper."

38

I looked at my cousin. "Cass, are you coming?"

"No." She jerked her chin at Maura. "I don't trust the pair of them."

"Xavier will stay here with them." I turned to him. "Is it true? Is the ghost out there in the hallway?"

He inclined his head. "She's right, but you should take Cass with you."

Cass made an irritated noise. "I don't appreciate being ordered around."

"C'mon." I beckoned her to follow me. "It'll be fine."

She gave Maura a last scowl before she marched out of the ballroom to join me. I saw the ghost immediately, hovering in the entryway to another downstairs room. Bailey shrank away when she saw our approach, and caution urged me to tread carefully so as not to frighten her away again.

"Don't worry," I told her. "I'm not going to harm you."

"It's not you I'm worried about." Her gaze flickered towards Cass. "Why are all these people here?"

"We're here to help you." I halted in front of her. "We're no friends of the people who lived here."

Bailey's nervous expression didn't abate, her attention landing on the open ballroom door. "What *are* those people? They're so... cold."

"Don't worry about them," I said. "Listen—you said you were looking for a friend. Do you remember the last time you saw them? How long ago?"

"I don't know." She spoke quietly. "It's all a blur. She wasn't here when I woke up like... like this."

She does know she's a ghost. I'd suspected she hadn't been familiar with the magical world when she died, but I imagined it was hard to ignore the obvious when one woke up alone in a gutted house with the sudden ability to walk through walls.

The question was, Why her? Why'd she come back, and how had she lingered so long after her death?

"When was that?" Cass broke in, impatient. "You're dead, but you know how to tell the time, don't you?"

I gave my cousin a warning look then returned my attention to the ghost. "Ignore that question. When you first came to this house, who gave you the address? Who invited you?"

"Nobody," she said tremulously. "Someone at my college was giving out invitations, and I got curious enough to grab one."

She was a normal. I'd thought so, but she must have gained some awareness of the magical world after being invited to a vampire's home—and dying there.

"Which college?" I queried.

"K-Kingshill."

The name rang an alarm in my head. Kingshill was the name of *my* old sixth-form college, which Laney and I had attended together. "Did you ask where they got the invitation from?"

"I don't know. I didn't ask." Her voice trembled. "Wynn wanted to come too. She's… dead, isn't she? It's my fault."

I attempted to soften my tone. "I haven't seen your friend. She might have gotten out."

"Or not," Cass said. "Were you aware that you were going to a vampire's house, or did you find out later?"

Bailey shrank away, her transparent face paling even more. "No… I didn't know. It seemed like a joke. It still does. Are you—are you with them?"

"No, we aren't." A pang struck my heart. "In fact, we're the ones who drove them away from here, but I didn't know that anyone was left behind. Do you remember the night that you came to the party?"

"I do." She squeezed her eyes shut. "I… I was supposed to

meet Wynn outside, but she never showed up, so I went into the house alone."

Oh boy. "Then what happened?"

"It all went wrong." She gulped. "At first, it was fun. There was wine—really strong stuff—and a bunch of people from school were here, but at the end of the night, things got… rowdy."

"And bitey?" Cass guessed.

Bailey gulped. "I was trying to get away from the shoving, but someone grabbed me, and… and bit me."

"Was that when…?"

"When you died?" Cass finished.

The ghost flinched. "No. I didn't realise what had happened at first. I was looking for Wynn, and I thought I saw her in the corridor, but it was *dark* in here, and cold, and… and someone had locked the front door."

A shiver trailed down my spine. "What then?"

"I don't remember." Her voice was a ragged whisper.

"But do you remember a fire?" Cass asked.

My heart lurched though I knew rationally that her death couldn't have occurred the night of the fire.

"Not then," the ghost said. "I… I do remember the fire, but I was already like… like this. I was hiding from *them* when I saw the flames."

"Were you?" Cass narrowed her eyes. "You did know that nobody could see you?"

"Cass, that's not helping."

"They could," Bailey whispered. "They chased me, but I escaped through… through the wall. That's when I knew I was d-dead."

The vampires could see her? Some of them must have been witches or wizards when they were still alive if they had the ability to see ghosts, though they couldn't use magic to banish the dead.

The question was, had her death been part of a vampire transformation gone wrong or an intentional murder? And what had happened to the others who'd been at the party that night? Those, I suspected, were questions a single ghost couldn't answer.

"Have you seen any of *them* since the fire?" I asked. "The ones who hosted the party?"

"No." She looked down at the floor. "No, but I've been hiding every time anyone comes into the house."

"Really," Cass said flatly. "I'm not sure I believe you."

"Why not?" I asked my cousin. "She's clearly not with the Founders."

"You don't seem like someone who was unaware the magical world existed until you wound up in a vampire's house," she said. "How long were you sneaking in and out of this world before you got yourself killed?"

The ghost's face crumpled. "I'm not lying."

"Really, Cass?" I hissed at my cousin. "What was that in aid of?"

"I don't like how knowledgeable she is," she said, while Bailey began to sob. "Ghosts are usually way more clueless about the circumstances of their death. A lot don't know they're even dead at all."

"She's been here a while."

The ghost had had plenty of time to adjust to the strange new reality of the world she'd stumbled into after her death.

"Oh, now you've done it," I added.

Sobbing hysterically, Bailey flew upward through the ceiling and vanished from sight.

Cass gave a shrug. "That was always going to happen. I think she sensed the sage in my pockets."

"You brought sage?" I asked. "Why?"

She shrugged. "A precaution. I brought a whole pack of

herbs I might need, plus firedust and other possible weapons."

"You thought we might run into the Founders again?" I turned back toward the ballroom. "What now? We could summon her again…"

"Feel free," Cass said. "I have more questions. For a start, if she died here, where's her body?"

"Is she likely to answer?" Asking that question of an already traumatised ghost probably wouldn't get us anywhere either. "We can look around and see if we can find anything."

Cass approached the ballroom again. "If you like."

We found the two Reapers having an intense staring contest, while Mart hovered upside-down and blew at the chandelier, causing the silvery decorations to jangle like bells.

"Rory," Xavier said, "did you learn anything new?"

"The ghost said she was bitten and presumably died from the shock," I explained. "It wasn't the same night as the fire, but I'm guessing she wasn't the only one the Founders killed. Also, Cass pointed out we don't know where her body is."

"That doesn't mean it's here in the house," Maura said. "Ghosts sometimes haunt places miles away from where they were buried."

"She was killed by the Founders who owned this place," Xavier pointed out. "I doubt they'd have taken her body too far from here, to avoid drawing suspicion."

"She wasn't sure whether any of them came back after the fire," I added. "She said she hid whenever anyone entered the house, because some of the vampires were able to see her."

"Are you sure her body wasn't burned in the fire?" Maura asked.

"If it was in the house… maybe." I shuddered. "But if the

ghost's here for unfinished business, that might include finding her body too."

The notion of combing the Founders' house for dead bodies didn't appeal in the slightest, but the Reapers' abilities only let them find spirits, not the mortal remnants of the dead. If the Founders had killed multiple normals inside this house, their families and loved ones would have no idea what had happened to them.

The grand old house contained over a dozen rooms aside from the ballroom, so our group split up to search each floor. While the Reapers went upstairs, Cass and I went from room to room on the lower floor.

"This is a waste of time," she griped. "I can guarantee they cleaned the place out. Besides, if there were bodies in here when the fire broke out, they'll have been burned to ashes."

"It's worth searching anyway." I opened a door that turned out to lead into a cloakroom. "There might be a hidden room or passageway somewhere. The house is certainly big enough for one."

"Nothing in here." Mart came drifting through the wall next to the cloakroom, making me jump. "Except dust. I guess they didn't want to be *that* obvious about where they hid their skeletons."

"Have you already finished searching upstairs?"

"Yep," he answered. "Even the attic's empty. They're the dullest vampires on the planet."

I dropped my gaze to the floor. "Can you do me a favour and have a look underneath to see if there's a basement underneath our feet?"

"Can I do *what?*" He gave a shocked gasp. "Would you ask a *living* person that question?"

"No, because you're dead," Cass said because she just had to.

Mart replied with a wail of despair and vanished through

the nearest wall. A moment later, his sister hurried up to join us.

"Did you hurt his feelings?" Maura guessed. "Watch it. He might drop a chandelier on your head."

"Can *you* check if there's a basement?" I asked her.

"There isn't," Xavier answered from behind Maura. "I checked."

We hadn't found any bodies, either, so our small, mismatched group gathered on the gravel path outside the front door. Mart was the last to leave the house, and he pointedly kept his distance from Cass and me, his nose in the air.

"There's always the garden," Maura said. "Burying the bodies is easier than locking them in a spare room."

"I'm not digging up the Founders' lawn," Cass said flatly. "Forget it."

Hmm. Maybe she was more bothered by this place than I'd thought. I had to admit I was glad to get away from the smell of burning and the unpleasant memories stirred up by being back in that house. I had no intention of coming back, but for that reason, I wanted to ensure we hadn't missed anything.

"If any new vampires were buried underground, they'd have clawed their way out or starved to death by now," Maura said. "Might as well check while we're here, though."

She found a rusty old gate at the side of the manor. It led to the back garden, where the once-pristine lawn was now neglected and overgrown. I fought a shiver at the memory of the vampires fleeing the fire while we made our own narrow escape from the flames.

"You know, we never did find out if Evangeline caught all the escaping vampires," Xavier murmured. "She wouldn't admit to having lost their trail, would she?"

"No... I'm not sure if she even caught Carlos Verdant."

I'd never asked. The details of that night occupied a prime spot in my nightmares that I didn't need to embellish with tales of Evangeline's vengeance, but now that my feet were planted back on their property, every bush seemed to conceal a fanged menace.

Don't be absurd, Rory, I told myself, studying the lawn instead. The soil was damp from recent rain and made it difficult to work out if anyone had dug any recent holes.

"I don't see any bodies," Cass announced. "They probably threw her in a field somewhere. Not too many people live out here."

I wasn't so sure about that, but I had to admit that I drew the line at trekking through every nearby field in search of human remains.

"Enough people live here to have heard the noise," Maura said. "Which makes me wonder how one ghost made enough of a racket to alert all the local farmers."

"There might have been other ghosts too," I suggested. "They'd have gradually disappeared over time."

"Hmm." Her mouth flattened into a line. "I don't know. This place gives me the creeps, and not in the typical haunted-house way. It's suspicious enough that Bailey's ghost has stuck around for as long as she has, given that she was a normal before she died."

"There's no rule saying someone has to be magical to turn into a ghost," I reminded her. "She died amongst para-normals."

"She also seems more adept than I'd expect of someone who gained most of her knowledge of the magical world after death," she said. "She died in a traumatic manner, but she doesn't act like she did."

"I don't know. She seemed pretty freaked out," I said. "And she can't do much harm as a ghost, can she?"

"I wouldn't speak too soon," Maura said. "Where'd you come from, anyway? You're local to the area, I take it?"

"Ivory Beach," I replied. "On the coast."

"Oh." Her expression turned guarded. "That's the town with the library?"

"Funnily enough, it is," Cass put in. "Been researching, have you?"

"What?" Maura said. "I thought it was a popular destination for anyone with an interest in rare books."

"Are you one of those people?" Cass asked.

"Might be," Maura said. "What's it to you?"

"We live in the library," I supplied. "If you want to find a book, rare or otherwise, we're the people to ask."

"Right." She eyed Cass, who looked stonily back.

"Whether you're coming to Ivory Beach or not, I have to tell my boss about you," Xavier said. "Sorry. It's a precaution."

Maura's shoulders slumped. "If you must, but I don't have time to sit through a lengthy interrogation. I'm only out of town for a weekend, and then I need to go back home first thing on Monday morning."

"Where is home?" I asked curiously.

"Hawkwood Hollow."

The name didn't ring a bell, but I still wasn't familiar with a lot of the magical communities elsewhere in the country. While I wasn't entirely certain she'd told the full truth, it was hard to imagine someone with nefarious intentions tolerating a ghost like Mart following them around.

"You might as well come back to Ivory Beach today," I said. "We have so few tourists that you'll have the pick of any rooms at the local inn."

Mart joined his sister, having apparently gotten over his sulk. "We'd be delighted to. I want to check out that library."

"We're not open until tomorrow." And that would depend

on whether the others had managed to get Aunt Candace out of whatever mess she'd ended up in before we left.

"We can wait until morning," Mart said. "Right, Maura?"

Maura, who looked as though she regretted even having mentioned her interest in the library, gave a faint sigh. "We'll see."

"Come on," Cass said. "I'm interested to see how the Grim Reaper reacts when you show up in town."

I was glad to turn my back on the Founders' house, but first, I had to find my familiar. Jet turned out to be hiding behind a hedge, and while I was coaxing him out, Cass used a transportation spell and disappeared. I urged Jet to fly back to the library by himself then joined Xavier.

"Are you going to follow Maura?" I whispered to him. "Through the afterworld?"

"That's the plan." His gaze skimmed over me. "You'll be all right?"

"Of course." I got out my wand. "I'll see you there."

The country lane vanished in a wave of my wand, to be replaced by the sloping high street. A few feet away were the gates to the local cemetery, but it wasn't Xavier who waited outside. Instead, Evangeline greeted me with a fanged smile.

I started at the sight of the vampires' leader. "Ah! Sorry. You surprised me."

"So did you," said Evangeline, who did not look surprised in the least. "I was expecting to find you in the library."

"Why did you want to come to the library?" It was fully

dark by then, which gave the cemetery an even eerier appearance. *Where's Xavier? And Maura?* "Why're you here? To see the Grim Reaper?"

"No," Evangeline said. "Not him."

"Really?" Xavier himself approached, his eyes narrowing. "Were you looking for me?"

"Or me?" Cass walked downhill toward us, folding her arms across her chest.

"No, this is merely a lucky coincidence." Evangeline's gaze flicked among the three of us. "While you're here, you might as well tell me about your visit to the Founders' house."

I didn't need to ask how she'd known where we'd been, but Cass's stubborn expression indicated she had no intention of talking. *As for Xavier...*

"Where is she?" I whispered to him, meaning Maura.

He shook his head in answer while Evangeline's expression grew more curious. "Well? What did you find?"

"We found a ghost of one of the Founders' victims," I replied. "But we didn't find her body although we searched the whole house."

"Interesting," she said. "Did the ghost have anything pertinent to say?"

"She was killed at one of their gatherings, before the fire," I explained. "I guess someone got overexcited and bit her and then didn't want to deal with the hassle of training up a new vampire.

"Or she was lying," Cass added.

"She might have been," I acknowledged, "but she was a normal before she was turned into a vampire. She was terrified. She also claimed she was looking for a friend of hers who was supposed to be at the house, but we didn't find anyone else. We didn't find any bodies either."

"Obviously, the Founders wouldn't leave evidence

behind," Cass said. "If you ask me, the ghost was there to make sure nobody came looking."

"I'm not sure she was alone." I addressed Evangeline. "The rumours you heard... Did they sound like the locals heard more than one ghost?"

"Now, I'm no expert on the echoes of the deceased," she said. "On that subject, did I hear someone mention a Reaper?"

"Not aloud," Xavier said frostily. "However, yes, there is a rogue Reaper in the area."

"*That* is intriguing," Evangeline said. "What's a Reaper from outside the region doing here, I wonder? Were they here to meet with the house's owners?"

Xavier's expression stilled. "What does that mean? The house has been empty for weeks."

"The Reaper claimed to be running a ghost blog." That seemed a harmless enough detail to mention. "She didn't seem to know anything about the Founders, either."

"Yet it seems she gave you the slip," Evangeline said, her tone amused. "Did you intend to report her to your boss, Reaper?"

"Yes," Xavier said tersely. "Once I've established why you're interested in talking to Rory."

Whoa. It wasn't like Xavier to be that blunt, though even the leader of the vampires was hardly threatening to an apprentice Reaper.

Before anyone else could speak, a high-pitched laugh sounded from behind the cemetery wall. "I thought I heard your voice, Evangeline."

Both Xavier and I started when another vampire sidled out of the cemetery, moving with the easy grace of the undead. She held the same otherworldly beauty as any vampire. Her features suggested Asian heritage, and her pale face was framed by straight jet-black hair. Her eyes, weirdly enough, were violet. Contacts? Or some vampire quirk I didn't know of yet?

"Come on, Evangeline," the newcomer said. "Introduce me to your friends, won't you?"

Whoa. This vampire must be close to Evangeline if she dared to speak to her in such a familiar manner, but why would she have been visiting the Grim Reaper? At least I assumed that was why she'd been in the cemetery.

I also hoped she hadn't heard too much of our conversation. The vampire's gaze skimmed across my face, and I avoided catching her eye, hoping that my inmost thoughts remained under lock and key.

"I am Victoire," the vampire said. "*You* must be Aurora."

"Ah… yes." I risked a glance at Evangeline, who wore an expression more akin to someone confronted with a mouldering old sandwich found behind a sofa than someone who'd been reunited with an old friend.

Victoire addressed Cass next. "And one of the cousins."

The stark incredulity on Cass's face might have amused me under any other circumstances. "One of the cousins?" she said acidly.

"And the Grim Reaper's apprentice," Victoire went on, undeterred. "Excellent. I've been looking forward to meeting all of you."

"No," Evangeline said in sharp tones. "I specifically invited you to my home, and yet you decided to spurn my invitation."

"I simply wanted to catch up with an old friend." She gave a delicate laugh.

"You're *friends* with the Grim Reaper?" The notion of the grumpy Reaper befriending anyone was too bizarre not to acknowledge, let alone a vampire.

"Oh, he and I go back a long way," she said with utter obliviousness to Evangeline's murderous aura. "Though that's par for the course when one is immortal. There are ways to avoid interacting with the others, of course, but I've never been one for seclusion. Neither have you, right, Evangeline?"

Tension laced the air. With Evangeline's coiled fury lurking beneath the surface, I didn't quite have the courage to ask more questions about how they knew one another, not when the next person to speak might end up skewered.

The tension broke when the Grim Reaper's shadowy figure loomed over the fence. "Xavier, come in here."

His apprentice turned toward him. "The other Reaper escaped. Do you want me to find her?"

"Now." That single word carried the weight of a ten-ton anchor. Even I swayed toward the cemetery, and Xavier gave me a brief apologetic look over his shoulder before his boss's shadow swallowed them both.

Someone isn't happy. Evidently, the Grim Reaper didn't feel the same about the vampire's supposed friendship as Victoire herself did, unless it was the other Reaper's escape that'd caught his ire.

"He's so *grumpy,* isn't he?" Victoire spoke as though commenting on the personality of a puppy instead of an angel of death. "Aurora, I can see why you picked the other one."

I didn't even know what to say to that. A not-insignificant part of me wanted to make an excuse and run like hell, but I also wanted to know how on earth she'd lived for so many centuries if she made a regular habit of annoying other prickly immortals.

"Victoire," Evangeline growled, "if you've quite finished here, I would invite you to come with me."

"Don't be like that," Victoire said. "It's been decades since we last saw one another. This should be a night of cele-bration!"

"Have you forgotten the circumstances of our last parting?" Evangeline spoke in tones more suited to a pronouncement of a death sentence than a warm greeting, but again, Victoire ignored the warning signs.

"Really, this is unnecessary," Victoire said. "There was that nasty business a few years ago, but everyone thought the collectors would be the future of *all* vampires back in those days, didn't they?"

"Not all of us did," Evangeline said. "I'll thank you not to rewrite our history. My memory is as sharp as it ever was."

"Ah, but we both took different lessons away from that little debacle, didn't we?" Victoire went on. "If not for the collectors, we'd have even fewer of our misplaced possessions back in our hands, where they belong."

Is she talking about the Founders? Evangeline's mouth opened wider with every word she spoke, exposing more of her pointed teeth.

Cass caught my arm and hissed, "Come on. We don't want to get dragged into this."

"No, but..." My curiosity warred with the instinct to get the hell away, and the latter won out. Turning my back on the vampires, I let Cass steer me down the high street.

"That one's even less trustworthy than Evangeline is," Cass said in a low voice. "And she has no boundaries about reading thoughts. She'd have gotten every one of the library's secrets from your mind if we'd stayed any longer."

"Still."

Unlike Cass, I didn't have a magical pendant that stopped the vampires from reading my thoughts. She'd taken offence at the idea of living in the same house as a vampire who could invade her privacy, and I'd been happy to make the compromise to have a little peace. Of course, with Laney in a coma, she didn't need to wear the pendant all the time, but I assumed she was keeping up the habit.

Back at the library, Aunt Adelaide came hurrying to meet us. "Oh… Rory. Cass. I wondered where you two had gone."

"Sorry I didn't have time to leave a note," I said. "Erm, did you manage to rescue Aunt Candace?"

"We did," my aunt replied. "I thought Xavier was busy this evening."

"That's why I went with her," Cass supplied. "He's being chewed out by his boss for letting a rogue Reaper slip through his fingers."

"A rogue *what?*" Estelle came hurrying across the lobby. "What have you two been doing?"

"We went to the Founders' house…" I trailed off when the colour drained from her face. "I thought you knew."

"I saw Cass leaving the library earlier, but she moved too fast for me to ask where she was going," she said. "That means… you didn't go alone, did you?"

"I followed Jet," I clarified. "He's been a little overeager to help me now that Aunt Candace doesn't seem to want to listen to his gossip any longer. When Xavier mentioned he couldn't make it, Jet flew off to the house. I couldn't just leave him."

"Of course not." Estelle's expression softened into its usual smile. "Wait, did you say you found a *Reaper?*"

"Not a rogue one," I added. "She was looking for ghosts, and… well, we found one. A victim of the Founders. I think she's the source of the rumours that Evangeline heard, but the poor ghost has been hiding from the vampires the whole time."

Cass made a sceptical noise. "Her story doesn't add up."

"In what way?" Estelle asked. "She's a ghost of someone they killed. There's a limit to how deceitful she can be, isn't there?"

"This Reaper, on the other hand…" Aunt Adelaide said. "She isn't local, I'm guessing."

"No, and it turned out that Xavier's boss sent him to catch her, and that's why he couldn't come with me," I told them. "She claimed to be helping out with a friend's blog on haunted houses."

"Except for the part that she was in the Founders' house," Cass said. "I don't buy her claims that she hadn't heard of them beforehand."

"She said she heard the name," I recalled. "She didn't know they were vampires."

"Where is the Reaper now?" Aunt Adelaide asked.

"She ran off," I said. "Through the afterworld, so I don't expect we'll see her again. Xavier got reeled in by his boss on the way back, so he might end up being sent to chase her down."

"Probably for the best," Estelle said. "You aren't planning any more trips to the Founders' house?"

I shook my head. "No, but it was Evangeline who made the suggestion, and she's tied up. Another vampire showed up to visit her, one who didn't exactly have a sensible level of respect towards the local vampires' leader."

"What?" Estelle asked. "Another vampire? Who?"

"She's called Victoire," I replied. "She and Evangeline had a contentious history, from what I gather, and she responded to Evangeline's offer of a visit by dropping in to see the Grim Reaper instead."

"Yes, Aunt Candace doesn't have a monopoly on poor decisions today," Cass said. "Also, a vampire who can annoy Evangeline and keep her head isn't someone we want to stand within biting distance of."

"Especially if she's been doing the same to the Grim Reaper." Aunt Adelaide tutted. "I'd stay away from both of them until this vampire has left town."

"Or gets herself shut in a coffin," Cass added.

"Weren't you interested in what she said?" I queried. "It

sounded… Well, it sounded like she had some history with the Founders, not just with Evangeline."

I was far from experienced in the nuances of the way the immortals interacted with the rest of the world, let alone with one another, but surely, Evangeline wouldn't have invited a *Founder* into her home.

"They're both vampires, Rory," she said. "Of course they have a history with the Founders. Doesn't mean they'll share the details with us mere mortals."

"Isn't it suspicious that she showed up in town right after I asked Evangeline for help with Laney?" I knew that'd get a reaction out of her and was braced when she levelled me with a glare.

"Did that vamp strike you as benevolent enough to help us mere mortals?" Cass asked. "No, let her play her games with Evangeline, and hope that our esteemed vampire leader manages to coax out her secrets before staking her to a tree."

Without waiting for a reply, she stalked off with her nose in the air, presumably back to Laney's room.

"Sounds like this vampire has a death wish," Estelle remarked. "Or undeath wish. You ran into her on the way back?"

"Yes—Evangeline claimed to be on her way to the library to look for me," I explained. "Instead, her friend showed up at the cemetery and stole her attention."

"I see." Aunt Adelaide pursed her lips. "She certainly seems a disruptive force, this Victoire. Acquainted with the Founders, is she?"

"She might be." *Don't get your hopes up, Rory,* I repri-manded myself. "She can't be a present member, given that she also claimed to be friends with the Grim Reaper."

"That'll be the day," Aunt Adelaide said. "Trouble, the lot of them are. The vampires, that is. Founders or otherwise."

I know. I'd happily have stayed far away from all of them if they hadn't been Laney's only hope. Opting for a change of subject, I asked, "What happened with Aunt Candace, anyway? I assume she's not stuck in a wall any longer."

"She'll tell you all the details at dinner, I expect."

I was too exhausted after our trail of misadventures to deal with another, so I opted to wait. When we gathered around the dinner table, Aunt Candace wasn't her usually vibrant self. Her notebook and pen hovered at her side, the same as usual, but her gaze remained fixed at a point in the distance, and she hardly seemed conscious of the rest of us as she picked at her food. Even her pen's scribbling on the note-book page seemed half-hearted, and she occasionally lifted her head toward the ceiling with a contemplative look on her face.

"Everything okay?" I asked her between bites of mashed potato. "I hear you had an eventful evening."

"Oh, it was wonderful." A dreamy air came over her. "I became one with the room itself."

"I think she left part of her brain behind when she got stuck in the wall," Cass muttered from across the table.

"There's no reason to mock me," my aunt said petulantly. "I solved my mother's riddle. Isn't that worthy of a cele-bration?"

"You don't look as if you're in a celebratory mood." I watched as Estelle and Aunt Adelaide exchanged raised eyebrows. "How'd you get stuck in the wall in the first place? I assume you didn't do it on purpose."

"Such a limited imagination," she said. "My heart's desire is to get into that room. When I wrote that desire upon the door with my own hand, the room was able to grant my wish. Do you see?"

I tried to get my head around that one. "You wrote on the door... and then what?"

"It sucked her in," Estelle added. "I think the room interpreted her desire to enter the room as a desire to... well, become part of the room itself."

"I *did* enter the room," Aunt Candace insisted. "I was right there."

"What else was inside the room, then?" I asked, curious despite myself as to whether she'd gotten any solid answers out of her narrow escape.

"Notebooks," she announced. "Countless notebooks piled in the centre of the room."

"Notebooks?" I echoed. "That's what you found in the room? Nothing else?"

"Clearly worth the risk." Cass gave an eye roll. "That's what Grandma set up a multilayered riddle to keep us from touching?"

"The notebooks might have contained the secrets of the universe," Aunt Candace said. "Unfortunately, in the state that I was in, I was unable to open any of them."

Cass snorted. "Because you didn't have hands when you became part of the wall. Still doesn't seem worth the risk, personally."

"You would say that," she said. "You're too serious. That's your problem."

"Aunt Candace, being fused with a wall is alarming even by the library's standards," I said. "I think we're all justified in being a little concerned. And do you not remember the time you lost your memory?"

"Vividly. Well, in a manner of speaking, given the unfortunate side effects." Her usual cheerfulness was back, along with a hint of mischief that suggested her misadventure had spawned a dozen new ideas. "Where have *you* been all day? Not doing anything interesting, I assume."

"For your information, I went to the Founders' old house," I replied. "The one I set on fire."

"And you didn't invite me?"

"You were stuck in a wall."

"Right." She pursed her lips. "I suppose you can be forgiven for the lapse."

"I thought you weren't interested in anything but that corridor."

"My interests know no bounds."

I don't doubt that. Frankly, the mysterious room on the fourth floor was the least of my worries. With another vampire in town who knew the Founders, it wouldn't be long before their attention landed on me again.

Or before they found out that I might need their help to save Laney.

6

After her escape from Xavier the previous day, I didn't expect to see Maura again for a while, but I thought wrong.

The next morning brought a shower of heavy rain and a general sense of malaise hanging over the library. I'd slept badly, my dreams haunted by Reapers and vampires and ghosts in the Founders' old house.

Estelle kept yawning too. "I was up late, making calls for the Halloween event," she explained as we prepared to open the library for the day. "I need to start decorating soon, but Sylvester popped all our ghost-shaped balloons."

"That owl."

I turned toward the stacks in case he was peering down from a shelf, but I hadn't seen much of Sylvester recently. He'd become even more elusive than usual after Aunt Candace's obsession with the missing corridor had taken over her life.

"I know." She yawned again. "I also know we're cutting it a bit close to the event, but I'm struggling to come up with a theme. I'm not in a Halloween mood, to be honest."

"Too much of that in real life." I knew how she felt. "I guess that after everything we've seen from the Founders recently, a vampire-themed masquerade would be a bit much."

"Exactly." Her expression brightened. "I was thinking something more harmless. Say, a treasure hunt with the local kids. But that might not attract as many people as a party would."

"Might be an idea." Admittedly, the thought of the library being full of hundreds of kids didn't lessen my desire to stay upstairs reading all night instead, but it was an improvement on anything related to the vampires. "Better than a ghost theme. Honestly, spirits aren't scary most of the time. They're sad."

"Like the one at the Founders' house."

I inclined my head. "I feel awful for her. A normal, pulled into this world by accident, and now, she's stuck haunting a vampire's house."

"I expect she'll move on soon," Estelle said. "All ghosts have to, in the end."

"I know." Yet her face had haunted my dream the previous night, and the knowledge that the Founders had harmed so many others made it difficult to look away.

"I can't believe Cass went with you," Estelle added. "Granted, lately, she's more unpredictable than Aunt Candace is."

"At least she hasn't turned herself into a wall recently." As I hadn't seen her today, I assumed Cass was either upstairs on the third floor with her animals or watching over Laney. "She practically dragged me away from that vampire friend of Evangeline's, which is probably for the best."

Estelle arched a brow. "Does Evangeline *have* friends?"

"Well... no," I replied. "She was surprisingly tolerant of Victoire's attempts to get under her skin, but I don't know how much of that was due to having known one another for centuries. Perhaps she's built up a tolerance. Or she planned to skewer her once they were behind closed doors."

"She has to keep up appearances in public, I suppose," Estelle said. "I'm glad you're okay. A Reaper, a ghost, and a vampire is a lot to deal with in the same day."

"Sorry I didn't tell you I was going to the Founders' house," I said. "I didn't expect Jet to take off like a rocket and fly there alone, and I didn't expect to run into anyone else, either."

"I know," she said. "Don't worry. I know Mum was a bit short with you, but she was mostly annoyed about Aunt Candace's latest escapade, not you."

"I get it," I said. "I'd like to hope Aunt Candace has learned her lesson, but given the way she was acting at dinner yesterday, I bet she hasn't."

"Nope," Estelle said. "Wouldn't surprise me if she's already back upstairs, scribbling a different request onto the door."

"It showed her a room full of notebooks." I thought back to her bizarre declaration. "What do you think was inside them? More magical codes?"

"I don't know," she said. "For all we know, the entire room was an illusion. Aunt Candace wasn't able to touch anything, and even the guardian didn't make an appearance."

"She doesn't seem bothered by that," I said. "What would it take to make her switch her focus to finding an antidote instead?"

"What antidote?"

I swivelled around to see Maura standing in front of the desk.

As my mouth fell open, she continued, "Hey, Rory. Wow, you really do live in the library."

Estelle took a startled step back. "Where did you come from?"

"The afterworld," I supplied. "This is Maura, the Reaper I met yesterday."

"And I'm her twin brother," Mart announced. "Nice place you've got here."

"I thought you left town." I should have known better, really, but she must've known the other Reapers would have already picked up on her presence. "What are you doing here?"

"Exploring." Mart darted around the desk, causing the books on the nearest shelf to lurch forward. "How do you keep track of everything in here?"

"We have a system—stop that." Estelle hastened to stop him from knocking the books over, while Maura stepped closer to the desk.

"Where's your cousin?" she asked me. "The charming one from the Founders' house?"

"Upstairs," I replied. "This is her sister, Estelle. And my aunt Adelaide's in the back. Listen, if you're here to make trouble, the library has a thousand curses set up to react against intruders."

"I'm not here to make trouble," she said. "I really did need to look something up in the library, and since I'm in the area, I figured I'd come and check it out. Mart, stop that."

Her brother, who was in the process of levitating a stack of books into the air, promptly dropped them all over the floor.

"So you are staying in town?" Estelle waved her wand to return the books into a stack, only for Sylvester to come swooping out of nowhere and knock them over again.

"What do we have here?" Sylvester hopped onto a shelf to peer down at Mart. "Anyone lost a ghost?"

"He can *see* me!" Mart exclaimed. "I've never been seen by an owl before."

"Sylvester is… special." I didn't quite dare to add any more detail than that, preferring to avoid the owl's talons. "Sylvester, Maura is looking for books on Reapers. We don't have any books here that'll be able to help her, do we?"

"We might." The owl rotated his head in the way that he did when trying to freak someone out.

Maura didn't even blink. "You must have thousands of books in here. One of them must be able to answer my question."

"Depends what you're looking for." I flicked my wand to levitate the books into a neat stack for Estelle to put back on the shelves. "Why not ask Xavier? If it's something Reaper-related you want to research, he's bound to know more than we do."

Maura grimaced. "I wasn't that keen on meeting his boss."

While Sylvester hooted with laughter, I said, "You do realise that he'll figure out you're here soon, if he hasn't already?"

"That's why I want to do this quickly." Maura glanced around the front desk. "Do you have… like, an index or something?"

"We do." I pulled out the reference list and unfurled the long stretch of parchment, but I was unsurprised to confirm that none of the subject codes written on the list were remotely related to the Reapers. "There's nothing on the afterworld in here."

"I figured, but I wanted to look up a spell," Maura said. "Or maybe a hex or curse. Whatever it is, it works on Reapers, which is why I'm interested."

"Works on Reapers?" *That* was unusual. "I doubt the Reaper Council would let information on possible weaknesses slip out of their clutches. It won't be in the same section as the regular spells or curses."

Reapers guarded their knowledge fiercely, and if she had links amongst the Council, it would surely be easier to get that information from them than from the library.

"They don't know," she said. "At least, I don't think the Council has any knowledge of this particular spell. It's complicated."

A thump sounded as the door swung open, revealing a familiar blond head, Xavier's. And if he hadn't knocked, he must think the situation was urgent enough to warrant barging in. He held his scythe in both hands, and hints of shadow swirled around his feet.

"I thought I sensed you appear," he said to Maura. "I had to answer a lot of questions from my boss after you gave me the slip yesterday."

"You told tales on me?" Maura sounded put out.

"I had to," Xavier said. "He already knew there was another Reaper present in the area, and he wouldn't have believed me if I told him we hadn't seen one another. I told him that you claimed not to be a rogue, but he wasn't convinced."

"He doesn't need to waste his time on me," Maura said. "Look, can I just get the book I need and go?"

"There isn't one," I said for Xavier's benefit. "She wants to know about spells that work on Reapers."

"That's not..." Maura trailed off. "I heard the library was the biggest source of magical knowledge in the region."

"It is." Xavier moved closer, shadows swirling around his palms. "Go on."

Maura took a reluctant step toward the door. "I also found out something about the Founders' victims, including the ghost we ran into in the house."

Bailey. The image of her terrified face came back into my mind's eye. "What did you find out?"

"When was this?" Xavier asked. "Before or after you ran off yesterday?"

"Wouldn't you have done the same?" Maura challenged. "After, for the record, but I'm not going to say any more to you if you're planning to have your boss use his scythe on me."

"I'll go with you," I found myself offering. "The Grim Reaper won't hurt someone who isn't intending to cause any harm, right, Xavier?"

He shook his head. "No, but this really isn't something that you should get involved with, Rory."

I didn't entirely trust Maura, either, but the fact that she'd come back to the library implied that she thought it was worth the risk. What else did she know about the ghosts we'd found at the Founders' house? If Sylvester hadn't chased her off, that meant she was no threat to the library, or to my family at least.

"I'll be fine," I said, trying to inject confidence into my words. "Estelle, I'll be back soon."

Concern flickered in her eyes, but she nodded. "All right."

Sylvester let out a cackle. "Let me know if he gets out his scythe."

"Come on." Xavier gestured toward the door. "We'll walk there on foot. No trickery."

Maura gave a sigh. "Fine, fine."

She pushed open the door and walked out. Xavier followed close behind, but she didn't vanish into the afterworld this time. She must have figured Xavier or his boss would catch her if she did, and even her ghostly brother accompanied her outside without raising an argument.

Xavier leaned over to whisper to me, "I don't think you should come with me. My boss was pretty irked yesterday."

"I know that," I muttered, "but I want to know what she learned about the ghost."

"She might be bluffing."

"She might," I agreed, "but if she was a threat, the library would have reacted against her. You know that."

"That doesn't mean my boss won't."

True, but his boss had nearly attacked *me* with his scythe at least once, and while my instincts urged me to stay away from the grumpy Reaper's domain, nobody else would help the forlorn spirit who'd been abandoned in the Founders' house. Maura, rogue or not, had reacted way too casually to things that would have freaked out any average person, but Reapers were far from average, even half-human ones like her.

When we reached the high street and the fence bordering the cemetery, Mart slowed to a halt. "I've changed my mind. I don't like Reapers."

"You *live* with one," I pointed out.

"Maura doesn't count," he said. "I'm staying behind."

"Thanks, but nice try," Maura said. "If I have to deal with this, so do you."

Xavier opened the gate, and the two siblings followed him through. I hesitated for a moment, then the image of the vampire from the previous day entered my mind and brought a surge of curiosity. *She knew the Grim Reaper.* No doubt he'd rather eat his scythe than tell me any of the details, but still.

We followed the gloomy path alongside the overgrown graves until we reached the Grim Reaper's home. It was pretty impressive how the large house somehow managed to avoid catching so much as a hint of sunlight no matter how nice the weather might be. On an overcast day like today, darkness shrouded every inch of the place. Mart whimpered and hid behind a tree, but Maura was unfazed, watching blank faced as Xavier unlocked the front door.

The Grim Reaper's shadowy form greeted us on the other side. He must have sensed us coming, and a chill raced down my skin even though I wasn't on the receiving end of his glare—and yes, it was definitely a glare. He might not have had any features aside from a vaguely humanoid form outlined in shadow and wielding a scythe, but every inch of him emanated menace.

"So this is our intruder." He lifted his hooded head to look past Maura's shoulder. "Is there a reason you are here too, Aurora?"

"We ran into each other in the Founders' old house, and I..." I trailed off when he turned away without listening to my reply and vanished into the gloomy hallway.

Xavier all but herded Maura into the house after him. Taking a deep breath, I entered behind the three Reapers, and the door closed on my heels. I fought the urge to huddle into my cloak, the chill leaching the warmth from my bones. The Reaper's house had no need for central heating, for obvious reasons, and my breath fogged the air as I followed Xavier through a door into a room that contained nothing except a long wooden table and several equally austere wooden chairs that nobody used.

Positioning himself at the head of the table, the Grim Reaper addressed Maura. "You're a rogue, by all definitions. There's no use in denial."

"I'm not acting against the council," she said. "That's the definition of a rogue."

"Incorrect," the Grim Reaper said. "The definition includes anyone who makes use of their Reaper powers without oversight in any capacity."

Huh? What was he playing at? I'd expected a face-off involving scythes, not semantics, and while I would hardly complain at the lack of violence, my body remained tense in case I had to run for the door.

"I have oversight," Maura replied. "Technically speaking. There's another Reaper in charge in my region, and I've interacted with others on the council too. They have no problem with me."

"You're a long way from home now, aren't you?"

"For a reason." Maura surveyed his shadowy face for a moment. "What if I were to tell you that someone has managed to develop magic that works against Reapers? Someone who isn't a Reaper themselves, that is?"

Chills emanated from the Grim Reaper's end of the table. "I'd say you were lying."

"I'm not," she said. "I've been on the receiving end of a spell that cut my Reaper powers off, and it was cast by a regular witch."

The Grim Reaper was silent for a heartbeat. "Prove it."

"That's kinda difficult, given that the witches in question are in jail," Maura replied. "Frankly, I'm not sure how they did it, either. It was set up like a booby trap, and a regular reversal spell got rid of the spell's effects."

His cutting stare didn't waver. "You came all the way here to research a mere practical joke?"

"It's no joke," Maura said. "Another witch had... Well, it was like an invisible shield that prevented me from using my powers on her."

"A shield?" His tone adjusted subtly. "Tell me more."

"Nothing to tell," Maura replied. "At a guess, it was some sort of talisman or amulet, because I didn't see her use her wand. I just couldn't touch her."

"Only a Reaper can counter another Reaper's powers."

"Trust me, this person is *not* a Reaper," Maura told him. "Even my ally's scythe bounced straight off her, and he's as baffled as I am. He *is* an official Reaper. Like I said, I've spoken to others."

"And you left your allies to deal with this supposed threat alone?"

"I have some time." She fidgeted. "Not much of it, admittedly. This witch is a menace to all of us, and I need to find out how to stop her."

"You expected to find answers in the library, did you?" he enquired.

"I heard the library was a major source of knowledge," she said. "I didn't count on running into another Reaper."

"Really." The Grim Reaper levelled a stare at her. "Why exactly were you in the Founders' house, then?"

Good question. I glanced at Maura, who looked more annoyed than frightened at the Grim Reaper's relentless questioning.

"Because I heard rumours," she said. "It's hard for me *not* to notice ghosts, and when I landed in the countryside near that house, I sensed… a lot of them."

"More ghosts?" My attention snapped over to her. "You mean the Founders' victims? I thought you didn't sense anyone else inside the house. Neither did Xavier."

"That's what I was going to tell you before," she replied. "It wasn't until you'd all headed back to Ivory Beach that I found at least a dozen other spirits wandering around the area. They were scattered across the neighbouring fields, which is why we didn't notice them earlier."

The Founders' victims. "Is that why the locals heard a load of noise from the house at night? The other ghosts are still there?"

"I was going to go back and check in daylight," she added, "but I didn't realise I needed to ask permission to look for ghosts outside of my own region."

I held my breath, expecting a reaction from the Grim

Reaper. Nobody else dared speak to him in that manner, but Maura seemed to have zero concept of the Reapers' hierarchy—that or she didn't care.

"Your attitude does you no credit," he said. "I assume, from your claims of urgency, that your demise would have unfortunate effects on anyone you might have left at home?"

"Yes," Maura replied. "A few Reapers would be pretty ticked off if I died, my dad being one of them."

I stared at her, curiosity stirring despite my better instincts. *Right. She's half Reaper. It's not all that surprising that one of her parents belongs to their ranks.*

"I think you'll find that not all Reapers agree with one another," he said. "If you haven't been honest with me, you can expect to meet a fate worse than those ghosts did."

"And if I have?" Maura said. "What then?"

"Then I'd advise you not to cross any more lines during your time here."

"You're letting me go?" she asked. "Really?"

"Really?" Xavier echoed her question. "You were convinced she was a dangerous rogue, I thought."

"Did you very much desire to Reap her soul, my apprentice?"

"Please don't," Maura said. "I'm not going to demand your help, but I could use some guidance while I'm here. This witch, the one who can counter a Reaper's powers... I think she had outside help."

"That is no concern of mine." The Grim Reaper waved a shadowed hand. "Don't make me reconsider letting you walk free."

Xavier looked as baffled as I felt. "Didn't you want me to keep an eye on her?"

"I thought that was a given, my apprentice," he said. "Don't let her leave your sight."

"Bet your girlfriend will love that," Maura muttered, just loud enough for me and Xavier to hear.

"I'll keep a close watch on her," Xavier told his boss. "And I'll find out what's up with those ghosts. I didn't realise there were others, but if she's right, that points to an anomaly in the afterworld."

"Bring a report to me as soon as you've investigated," the Grim Reaper ordered.

"I will." Xavier moved toward the door. "We'll go right away."

Hardly able to believe that we'd all got out of this unscathed, I gladly followed Xavier, and we left the Grim Reaper's house behind.

7

I exhaled in a sigh of relief when the Grim Reaper's door closed behind us. "That was lucky. Or weird."

"I'll go with the former." Maura stepped forward, and her brother came out from amongst the graves.

"Good, you're alive," Mart said. "How was His Grumpiness?"

"Not that bad, believe it or not," Maura said, flashing a smile at Xavier. "Your house is far nicer than my own local Reaper's, you know."

Xavier didn't smile back. "I don't know why my boss let you go, but I'm going to have to follow his orders to keep an eye on you."

"Maybe he's curious about those ghosts," I said doubtfully. "Maura, did you speak to any of them? You said they were in the fields near the house?"

"They ran off when I tried to approach them," she said. "As you'd expect. I don't know why that one was inside the house and the others weren't."

"Maybe that's where she expected to find her missing friend," I recalled. "If she's been hiding inside the Founders' house all along, she might not know there are other ghosts wandering around outside. And… one of them might be her friend too."

"Might be worth asking them," Maura acknowledged. "If you approach with caution. They're skittish, and I can't say I blame them."

"We never did find the bodies, either." I swivelled toward Xavier. "Ghosts normally stick around when they have unfinished business, don't they? Why would so many of them stay in a single region?"

"I don't know," he said, "but they're unlikely to show their faces when there are two Reapers nearby. I got the impression that my boss wanted me to banish them and save the bother of asking questions."

"Who else is going to help them?" I pushed open the gate, the tension lifting from my shoulders as we left the cemetery behind. "Certainly not the vampires. Which reminds me. Xavier, did your boss mention anything about his intriguing visitor yesterday?"

"No." His gaze flickered in Maura's direction. "He didn't."

If he'd appointed himself as Maura's official watcher for as long as she was in town, it would be kind of tricky to find any time to talk in private, and it was understandable that he wouldn't want to mention my entanglements with the Founders in front of her. At least Reapers couldn't read minds, but my curiosity about Evangeline's mysterious guest would have to remain unsatisfied for the time being. I'd been trying to save Laney for long enough that I was willing to seize on anything that might help, but it wasn't just Laney whom the Founders had hurt. *Look at that poor ghost.*

"Where are we going now?" Mart said from behind us. "To ambush some more ghosts?"

"Back to the library," I decided. "Maura, you haven't asked

my aunts about your mysterious Reaper-proof spell yet. They might be able to help."

My family members would also be relieved to find out that we'd all survived our encounter with the Grim Reaper unscathed. Nobody argued, so I led the way back across the square toward the library.

This time, Aunt Adelaide stood behind the front desk, not Estelle. "I wondered where you'd gone, Rory," she said. "Estelle had to make another call… Oh, hello, Xavier. And who's this?"

"This is Maura," I explained, "the Reaper we met at the Founders' old house."

Aunt Adelaide's expression darkened. "Is she, now?"

"The Grim Reaper vouched for her," I added. "But Xavier's here to keep an eye out for trouble."

"You ran into her at the Founders' house." Aunt Adelaide eyed Maura with uncharacteristic mistrust. "Why were you there, exactly?"

"Looking for ghosts," Maura replied. "We didn't know who the house actually belonged to at the time."

"We?"

"Us." Mart popped up and gave a bow. "It's charming to meet you."

Aunt Adelaide blinked at him. "You came with Maura? Ghosts aren't supposed to be able to travel far from their place of haunting."

Mart grinned. "Wow, you can *all* see me?"

"This is my brother," Maura told her. "Anyway, I wondered if you might have any books on spells that work against Reapers. Or people who've experimented with magic to create a similar kind of spell. Whichever sounds more relevant."

"Those are two vastly different things," Aunt Adelaide said. "Experimental magic is a niche area that you're more likely to be able to find useful information on from talking to one of our local university professors. Reaper-proof spells, on the other hand, are strictly the business of your own kind. If you're looking for someone who's created a spell designed to work against Reapers, you won't get very far here."

"I assume she's looking for examples of people who've tried the same in the past," I ventured. "It sounds like the person in question is using an amulet or a talisman since they didn't use a wand. Right, Maura?"

"Looked that way," she replied. "This witch—nasty piece of work—has been trying to get revenge on me for a while. Long story, but she's got hold of something that deflects my Reaper powers, and I'd rather be prepared when I next face her. I heard your library has more books on theoretical magic than anywhere else in the country."

"Really?" Aunt Adelaide cocked a brow. "You came all this way and somehow ended up in the Founders' house instead of the library?"

"I got distracted by ghosts. It happens to us Reapers a lot." Impatience filled Maura's voice. "Listen, I can only stay here for the weekend, and even that's pushing it. I wanted to see what I could find in the library during that window, but if you don't have anything useful, I'll go."

"We do, don't we?" I asked my aunt. "I mean, people have created spells before. And potions, magical objects... pretty much everything you can think of."

"Yes, but the sheer scope of that subject is beyond what I can explain in a weekend," my aunt said. "Like I said, you'd be better off asking one of the professors at the local university."

"Not sure about that," I muttered, thinking of our recent misadventures on the university campus. "They don't always know the answers either. What about Aunt Candace? *She's* created magical objects before."

She and my grandmother and my dad had worked

together to create the Spell Assistant and the magical translators that I'd used to decipher my dad's journal. Also, my grandmother had created the fourth-floor corridor itself.

"Candace is also currently out of trouble, and I'd prefer that she stayed that way," Aunt Adelaide said firmly. "Her own experiments, fortunately, have nothing to do with the afterworld."

"Never mind, then." Maura motioned toward the door. "We'll go…"

"Where, back to the Founders' house?" I asked. "Because if you need a non-Reaper to talk to the ghosts, I'll go with you."

"Not again." Aunt Adelaide pressed her lips together. "Rory… that house is bad news, like everything connected to the vampires."

"I know, but that ghost… she's alone in there."

"Not alone if there are other ghosts everywhere outside," Maura added. "Who exactly *are* these Founders, anyway? Nobody will give me a straight answer."

"Who have you been asking?" I asked in alarm.

"You," she replied. "And your boyfriend. Don't look so freaked out. I figured that if the vampires here are anything like the other ones I've met, they don't mingle with nonvampires much."

"No…" I trailed off, debating inwardly, then decided to plunge ahead. "The Founders are a group of knowledge-collecting vampires. They're primarily rich aristocrats, as you may have gathered from the state of their house."

Maura nodded. "I already worked most of that out for myself, but aren't *most* vampires ancient and terrifying? What makes this group so notorious?"

I threw caution to the wind. "Mostly their nasty habit of acquiring knowledge by torturing and extortion—and more recently, kidnapping and biting normals. Apparently for fun."

"Ah." She grimaced. "Knowledge, you say? What kind of knowledge?"

I shrugged. "Anything they think is valuable. We've been their targets several times in the past because of the library."

"I'm guessing that's what led to you burning down their house." Maura glanced at my aunt. "Look, I'm not trying to impose. I gather that you don't normally like Reapers. Believe me, I'm used to it."

"That's not it," Xavier said. "It's the fact that your story doesn't add up. If your priority is finding a way to overcome this witch, why did you let the local ghosts distract you so easily? And of all the ghosts to go after, why the ones in the Founders' house? There are other haunted buildings in the region that are far better documented."

"I doubt any of those other buildings has more than a dozen ghosts," she said. "They were everywhere, and if they were all the Founders' victims, I expect their loved ones probably want to know what happened to them."

"Yeah." I glanced at Xavier. "It's true, right?"

Bailey had said the original invitation to the Founders' gathering had come from someone at college—at the same sixth-form college *I'd* gone to as a teenager. I found it hard to look away from that connection, though I also didn't want to get into a discussion in front of Maura on how I'd once been a normal myself.

Before anyone could reply, Estelle walked into view. "Hey, Rory. The Grim Reaper didn't use his scythe on anyone, I take it?"

"No." I drew in a breath. "Estelle, can you look something up for me? The ghost we ran into in the house… I know the area she came from, so I wondered if her family knows she's missing."

"Sure." She held up her phone and typed the address I gave her. I could sense Maura watching me curiously, but I didn't elaborate on how I'd become familiar with that particular region. "What do you want, local news stories?"

"Please." I watched over her shoulder as she ran a search. A familiar face leapt out at me from a photo at the top of a news article from earlier in the summer, featuring a series of disappearances from the local college.

"That's the ghost?" Estelle blanched. "She's a kid. It sounds like her family's really worried about her… and she isn't the only one who's vanished, either."

"I know." Guilt churned inside me. "What should we do? We can't exactly call the police and say that we know where she is. Or where she died. There's no proof that we can give to normals that wouldn't get us into trouble."

"No, and it's not our place to," Aunt Adelaide said. "The Founders broke numerous laws when they captured normals, and it's equally illegal for us to get involved ourselves."

"You don't think Evangeline is going to be nice enough to call all those people's families, do you?" My hands clenched. "Estelle, how many victims are listed in that article?"

"At least ten." Estelle bit her lower lip. "Bailey's address is here too."

Maura craned her neck to see Estelle's phone screen. "Where?"

As Estelle held out her phone, my mind sharpened in recognition. "That's… that's not far from where I used to live."

Had the Founders picked that location on purpose, or was it mere coincidence? They'd been active in the area already when they showed up at my dad's shop, but I couldn't help wondering if their choice of human targets had been intentional as well.

"Really?" Estelle eyed me with concern then skimmed through the article. "The disappearances occurred before the

Founders' house was abandoned. There haven't been any recent incidents, it doesn't look like."

"But their victims were never found." I didn't know what the right move was, but Laney was one step removed from having been in a similar situation herself. How could I walk away?

"You want to speak to Bailey's parents?" Maura guessed. "That might end badly."

"I don't know, but someone has to act, and it sure as hell won't be Evangeline," I replied. "The vampires are supposed to police their own, but dealing with normals is way outside of her usual area."

"I guess we could drop by at Bailey's house before we speak to the ghosts," Maura said. "We can ask a couple of questions without mentioning Bailey's fate. Better not to, in my mind."

"Agreed." Xavier swivelled toward me. "Rory... what do you think?"

My mouth parted. "You think the ghosts will take off as soon as the pair of you show up, don't you?"

"Yes, and if you go, I'll come with you," he said. "Which means Maura is along for the ride."

"Don't forget me," Mart said. "*I* can talk to the ghosts."

"He can," Maura said thoughtfully. "But like you said, the ghosts aren't likely to trust either of us. I can see the benefits of asking Bailey's parents about her friend Wynn."

"You don't think Wynn's one of the victims?"

Admittedly, if Bailey had been haunting the house for weeks, she probably would've encountered her friend among the other ghosts.

"Estelle? Is her name in the article?"

"Wynn?" she echoed. "No. Nobody by that name is mentioned."

That means she's walking amongst normals, potentially

spreading stories of the Founders' house. "I think we should look for her."

"All right," Xavier said. "I'll go through the afterworld… if Maura agrees to behave herself."

"I've nowhere else to go." Maura shrugged. "You'll just have to trust me."

"I'll use a transportation spell," I decided. "Meet you there."

I hoped Maura wouldn't give him the slip again. It was a risk, but since she could theoretically vanish at any moment anyway, we'd have to rely on her sense of goodwill, if she had one.

I committed the address to memory and got ready to use a transportation spell. Fixing on a smile, I said to my family members, "Don't worry. I'll be back soon."

As the two Reapers—plus Mart—vanished, I waved my wand and pictured the area in which I grew up. The library disappeared, and cold air stung my face. I'd landed beside the river—the one I'd jumped into to escape the Founders the first time around, near the apartment building where I lived for the first miserable years after Dad's death.

I didn't like to spend too much time dwelling on those days, but I couldn't help suspecting that the Founders had picked out their victims based on their proximity to my old home in another attempt to dig in the knife. I *hoped* the fire at the house had put an end to their recruitment, but it was too late to save Bailey or her unlucky fellow normals.

Shutting a lid on the unpleasant memories, I found Xavier and Maura waiting for me on the other side of the bridge.

"We're in the right place, I take it?" Maura asked. "Mart, get out of the river."

Her brother surfaced from the water and splashed her. "Very drab, this place is."

"Yes, and we're going to see a pair of grieving parents, so please stop with the nonsense," Maura told her brother.

"I'm not sure we should speak to them," I admitted, some of my resolve having faded after the unwelcome reminders of my first narrow escape from the Founders. "Maybe we should look around first."

"You want to break into a dead person's home?" Mart asked. "How is that better than asking questions?"

"Technically, it's not breaking in when you don't touch the door," Maura said.

"That's illegal even for Reapers," Xavier said firmly. "We aren't breaking into their house."

"No, I didn't mean that either," I clarified. "Never mind. We'll ask some questions, like I said. I just forgot how... how ordinary this place is."

"You want to find out if she left any clues behind, don't you?" Maura asked me. "About who killed her."

"I know who killed her." What I didn't know was whether they were still active in the area, despite us having driven them out of their base. "Never mind. Let's go."

I also knew the area like the back of my hand, and in no time at all, I found the cul-de-sac lined with neat brick houses. Not a trace of a vampire was in sight, but I paused halfway down the row of houses and spied a young woman lurking outside a door that a second glance confirmed to be the house we needed. The woman was maybe seventeen, with dark cropped hair and a nose piercing.

"Excuse me?" I asked before I could lose what remained of my nerve. "Are you looking for Bailey's house?"

"You know her?" A frown appeared on her pale face. "You don't look familiar. You're too old to go to my school."

"My younger sister does," I invented. "She was wondering if... if they'd found her."

"No." Her eyes brimmed with tears. "I've been asking the

police every day, but they don't care. They say she ran away from home, but she wouldn't."

"No." Caution urged me to tread carefully, but I had a suspicion I knew who she was. "Was she invited to a party of any kind recently? My... ah, sister... She got the same invitation."

"Who?" Shock flitted across her face. "Yes, and so did I. I thought it was exclusive."

"Are you... Wynn?"

"How'd you know my name?" Her suspicion returned. "Who *is* your sister, anyway?"

"She... Look, it doesn't matter." I knew this was Bailey's missing friend, the one who'd escaped, and I didn't dare let her out of my sight. "You went to that house? The one way out in the countryside?"

She wiped her eyes on the back of her hand, leaving a trail of mascara. "Yeah. I got cold feet and left the party early. Then she... she never came home."

"How much of the party did you see?" I asked carefully. "Did you go into the house at all?"

"For a bit, yeah," she said. "They were weird rich aristocrats, the owners were. Why?"

"And did they give you anything?"

"Give us anything?" she echoed. "What, like drugs? There was something odd in the wine, I think, Bailey said. She was all giggly and high for days after the first party."

Vampire blood, perhaps. Yet she'd adeptly avoided mentioning any obvious red flags.

"If you left the party early, I assume you caught a glimpse of your hosts," Maura said from behind me. "Did they have more fangs than the average person?"

"What?" Wynn paled, staring at her. "What are you people up to?"

"Nothing." I held out a placating hand. "We were trying to

help you. Bailey, too. The people who owned that house…
Did you know them?"

She dropped her gaze. "I don't know anything. It was a
mistake even to take the invitation, but Bailey wanted to, and
I didn't want to let her down. Where is Bailey? You've seen
her recently, haven't you?"

"No," Maura said flatly. "You're better off going home."

"I know Bailey," she said tremulously. "She's my best
friend. Please. Something happened to her at that house…
right?"

"She's dead," Maura told her. "Sorry."

Without waiting for her words to sink in, Maura strode
away from the house. I hastened to follow, not wanting to be
left alone with a heartbroken normal and a list of questions I
couldn't answer. Wynn's sobs tugged at my heart as I ran out
of the cul-de-sac, Xavier close behind me.

"Maura, what *was* that?" I hissed at her. "She's a normal.
Plainly, she didn't know anything."

"You wanted Bailey's loved ones to know the truth, didn't
you?"

"Not like that."

"I don't trust her," Maura said. "I'm sure she must have
glimpsed more of the vampires than she let on. And how did
she get home after the party, considering the Founders'
home is out in the middle of nowhere?"

"A taxi?" I suggested. "You don't think she was telling the
truth?"

"I think she did get cold feet," Maura said, "but I don't
know if she's being entirely honest. Why would Bailey have
been so certain that she'd find her friend inside the house if
she supposedly left the party early?"

"I don't know. She's a ghost," I said. "She might be
confused or have forgotten. Same goes for the other ghosts,
come to that."

"You want to talk to them now?" she guessed.

"It was our original plan." Though it was probably a long shot to expect the ghosts to come close to *two* Reapers. I'd have to approach alone, and with caution.

"All right," Xavier said. "Whether she's in the know or not, Bailey's ghost has unfinished business."

Maura nodded. "And it's theoretically a Reaper's job to help souls move on."

Yeah... but I feel obligated to help too.

The Founders must know the chaos they risked causing by exposing our world to normals, let alone in such a violent manner. Yet they kept doing so, and they kept hurting innocent people in the process.

I refused to let them get away with it any longer.

8

Using a transportation spell to return to the Founders' house would have been a lot more pleasant than a trip through the afterworld, but for some reason, I found myself turning toward Xavier. "Take me with you?"

His mouth parted in surprise, but he nodded. "All right."

Maura looked at me curiously but didn't say anything as I took Xavier's arm. Darkness folded around us, and a moment later, we landed on a country lane near the Founders' house. Maura appeared a heartbeat after Xavier did, with Mart hovering behind her.

When the latter saw me shivering, he grinned. "What's true love if you can't enjoy a trip through the afterworld together? Very brave of you."

I offered him an eye roll and turned to his sister. "Whereabouts are the other ghosts you saw?"

"All around." Maura peered over the fence into the neighbouring field. "Or they were, but if a pair of Reapers gets too close, they're likely to disappear. We'll need to sneak up on them."

"I can find their general direction," Xavier said.

Darkness folded around us, causing me to shiver again, although the sensation was nowhere near as uncomfortable as being pulled *through* the afterworld. Maura and Xavier both lifted their gazes to stare into the distance, then the darkness vanished as swiftly as it had appeared.

"Over there." Maura pointed down the road, past the vampires' house. "They're all clustered around that field. Go ahead, Rory."

"All right."

I caught Xavier's eye, and he nodded, though he didn't look too pleased at the notion of me approaching the ghosts alone. If we wanted to talk to any of the spirits without them immediately being scared off, however, I didn't have much choice.

As I drew closer to the field they'd pointed out, I recognised the faint glow of a transparent ghost then a second glow and a third. The field backed onto the Founders' garden, with a brick wall separating the two, but the ghosts had clustered around one side of the field. I scanned the fence for the easiest route to climb over, but a sudden movement from the direction of the Founders' house drew my attention. Whatever it was, it'd moved quickly enough to leave nothing more than a blurred impression on my retinas.

Like a vampire.

"Rory?" Xavier called to me. "What's wrong?"

"I—" I spun back to the field, but the transparent figures had vanished. "What—where'd the ghosts disappear to?"

"They've gone?" Maura came jogging up to join me at the fence. "Huh. Weird."

"Probably because you just brought a group of Reapers into their field," Mart said from behind her. "Well done."

"They vanished before the Reapers caught up," I said. "I swear I saw a vampire. Or something equally fast."

"A vampire?" Xavier joined us, his expression darkening. "Where?"

I pointed over at the wall separating the field from the Founders' garden. "In there."

"I'll look." Maura scaled the fence into the field and began a determined march across the grass.

"So much for not freaking out the ghosts."

A vampire moving at top speed was difficult for the human eye to spot, and I could hardly blame the ghosts for scattering, but which vampire would come back to the house at this point? Maybe it'd been one of Evangeline's people.

I followed Maura, awkwardly climbing over the fence, and stumbled in the mud when I hit the other side. I didn't see any signs of the intruder. Nor the ghosts.

"Does this field belong to the same people who owned the house?" I asked Xavier, who'd joined me in a far more graceful manner.

"I assume it does," Xavier replied. "The ghosts picked this place to haunt for a reason."

Because this is where the vampires buried the bodies? The question arose unbidden, along with a chill of foreboding. Shaking off the unease, I crossed the field behind Maura. The rain made it tricky to stay upright. I skidded in a particularly wet patch of mud, and my gaze caught on a flickering movement in the field's corner. "What's that over there?"

If I hadn't spent nearly a year in my family's magical library, becoming adept at noticing the slightest trace of magic, I might have missed the telltale glimmer of a conceal-ment charm, a powerful one. When I drew closer, the cracks began to show, and the outline of a small building shim-mered against the air.

"Rory..." Xavier followed my gaze. "Is that what I think it is?"

"Yeah," I said quietly. "A concealment spell. A good one too."

"Is it?" Maura strode toward the invisible building and kicked at the air. The concealment spell popped out of existence, revealing a building maybe the size of a bicycle shed with a sloping roof and a single wooden door. The sole window was caked in grime, which made it impossible to see what was inside.

"Who hid this place?" I already knew the answer, but a thousand more questions sprang into existence in my mind.

"Let's see what the Founders didn't want anyone to find." Maura pulled out her wand and gave it a flick, and the door sprang open.

A horrible smell poured out, a mixture of rotten eggs and something decaying. I held my breath, fighting the urge to gag, and glimpsed a room full of cabinets and tables covered in bottles and jars. The darkness was too complete for me to make out their contents.

"Somehow, I doubt this is their secret beauty salon," Maura muttered as she walked in. "Unless they're really into hair dye."

I stepped inside and found a light switch, flicking it on. Dust stirred, making me cough, but the dim light shone upon the tables and cabinets and illuminated an array of potions whose purpose I could only guess at. My pulse raced. If the Founders had been experimenting in this room, might the antidote for Laney's condition be somewhere in here? I picked up a bottle, trying to read its label, but the ink had smudged.

"One four three," Maura read over my shoulder. "A code. None of the labels say what's actually in the bottles."

"There must be a way of identifying each of them." I scanned the room, and my gaze landed on a trapdoor in a corner. "What's that? Secret passage?"

"Let's see." Maura wasted no time in walking over to the trapdoor. "Probably a way to sneak out of the house if they ended up cornered."

"They didn't use it when the house caught fire."

"No, but who'd want to go underground in those circumstances?" Maura crouched down and pulled the trapdoor upward. "Yuck. It stinks like something died in there… Oh."

The quiet note at the end of her voice made the hairs on my arms rise.

Xavier glided across the room and came to a halt at her side. "Oh no."

"What?" A horrible possibility slid into my mind. "Is that where…?"

"Don't look, Rory."

I didn't need to. My mind conjured up images from my nightmares, and a violent shiver gripped my whole body. *Bailey. Her friends…*

"What's all this?" Mart came gliding across the room then let out a yell. "Murder!"

Still yelling, Mart fled the house. I followed him, my instincts kicking in and driving me into a flat-out sprint. Partway across the field, I forced myself to stop, bracing my hands on my knees to catch my breath. *I can't leave them there. If that's where Bailey and her friends' bodies were hidden…*

I jumped when Xavier appeared behind me and touched my shoulder. "Sorry, Rory. I'm sorry. I… I recognised Bailey and some of the other ghosts."

"Someone has to call the police," I mumbled. "We can't leave them here."

"I'll do it." He pulled out his phone. "You don't need to worry."

"Yes, I do," I argued. "Those potions… they aren't the sort of thing we want normals finding, are they? What're we supposed to do with them?"

Edwin's team covered only Ivory Beach, but this entire area was inhabited by normals, and I didn't know where their local police force was located. No doubt, that loophole had enabled the Founders to get away with their illicit activities to begin with, but I could only imagine what havoc might ensue if those potions ended up in the hands of more unwitting normals.

"Good point," Xavier said. "I'll ask Edwin about that too."

"Bet he'll be thrilled." I wrapped my arms around myself, shivering harder. If this brought some relief to the families of those poor people, it'd be worth it, but I couldn't help wondering why all the ghosts had vanished so suddenly.

And which vampire did I see?

———

An hour later, I was back at the library, sitting in the Reading Corner with a mug of hot chocolate in my hands. My hands were trembling a little, still, but I felt a little better now I was out of that horrible place. Xavier and Maura had gone to help Edwin's staff remove the contents of the lab and transport them somewhere safer, but I'd been unable to tolerate being around the Founders' house a moment longer.

"Those Founders." Estelle came and sat next to me. "They're even more twisted than I thought."

"Yeah." I'd told her and Aunt Adelaide everything, though Cass hadn't shown herself yet, and I hadn't got up the courage to walk into Laney's room so soon after seeing more results of the Founders' depravity.

As for Aunt Candace, she'd returned to the fourth floor to resume her efforts to get into the hidden room. I'd entertained the idea of trying to distract her by mentioning the mysterious potions we'd excavated from the Founders' house, but that was almost as likely to end in disaster as her attempts to get through the door.

"Sorry, Rory," Estelle said. "It must have been a shock, finding all those poor people."

"It was worse for the victims," I insisted. "I'm glad their families will be able to have closure, but they should never have been in that house to begin with."

"No." Estelle shook her head. "They shouldn't have. It's sick, what the Founders did, but at least we drove them away."

That didn't feel like enough, but I nodded and finished my hot chocolate. "I should help your mother with the returns."

"You've done enough today," she said. "Is Xavier coming back?"

"No… he has to watch Maura," I said. "His boss told him to keep an eye on her."

Well, Xavier had volunteered himself, but I was no closer to figuring out why his boss had had such an abrupt change of heart where Maura was concerned. Nor was I any the wiser as to the Grim Reaper's connection with Evangeline's mysterious guest, but I figured it was probably too much exertion to go and see the Grim Reaper or Evangeline after the day I'd had already. All the same, I wanted to do *something* useful.

"Good call," Estelle said. "Honestly, she might have had nothing to do with what you found in the Founders' house, but she seems like a magnet for trouble. If you ask me, you're better off staying away from her."

"She's going home by the end of the weekend anyway." Assuming she'd be content to walk away without answers. To change the subject, I asked, "How's the Halloween planning going?"

"It's an absolute disappointment," Aunt Candace

answered, stepping out from behind a shelf. "She isn't even going with the vampire masquerade theme."

"You're joking, aren't you?" I shook my head at her. "Nobody wants a vampire masquerade theme except for you."

"Also, Evangeline wouldn't approve," Estelle said. "No, we're doing a regular costume party instead. Something low-key."

"What a waste." Aunt Candace gave a sigh. "Halloween comes around only once a year, you know."

"You can dress up however you like," I told her. "Evangeline isn't attending, in all likelihood, so she won't chew you out for wearing a cape or plastic fangs."

I hope. I never really knew what to expect from Evangeline, nor did I know how long her mysterious new friend would be staying in town. Based on what I'd seen of Victoire's behaviour, a vampire-themed party run by humans would be right up her alley, assuming Evangeline hadn't lost her patience before then, of course.

"Why are you two sitting here alone?" Aunt Candace asked. "You look as if you're conspiring. I want in on it."

"There's no conspiracy." I took in a breath. "We found a bunch of bodies of the Founders' victims in a lab near their house."

"You found dead bodies and didn't tell me?" She sounded insulted. "*And* a lab? I'm shocked at the omission."

"They were normals, Aunt Candace," I said tersely. "They were brutally murdered by vampires. There's no book in that. It's just sad."

"No need for that tone," she said. "How was I supposed to know? Nobody tells me a thing."

"I thought you were upstairs," Estelle said to her. "You haven't been around today."

"And I shall continue to not be around." With a dramatic sweep of her dress, she vanished behind the shelves again.

"She's not going up to the fourth floor, is she?" I groaned. "I was probably too hard on her. She doesn't mean to be inappropriate, I know."

"Still, there's a time and a place for her nonsense," Estelle said. "Not that we need her turning herself into part of the interior decorating again."

"Do you think she did make progress with the corridor?" I asked. "I mean, theoretically, she *did* get into the room. Or the wall, anyway."

"Trying to make sense of it all makes my head spin." Estelle's brow wrinkled. "She said she saw notebooks inside the room, which will probably turn out to be written in *another* secret code. Not that she could actually touch any of them."

"That's probably what she'll try next." While there must have been method to the madness somewhere, I didn't particularly want to get ensnared in one of Aunt Candace's madcap schemes, but at least it would be a welcome distraction from the horror of what the Founders had done. "I'll go and apologise to her."

I made for the stairs, which curved around and offered me a view of Aunt Candace climbing ahead of me at speed. I didn't catch her up until the third floor, where she'd already made a beeline for the door at the back.

The door that led to the fourth floor was unremarkable except for its tendency to change colours, but its sudden reappearance had opened a new chapter in our already chaotic life in the library. The doors that lay on the other side were immune to the keys our family owned that worked everywhere else in the library and were guarded by a creation of my grandmother that was designed to fend off trespassers. I'd have thought having her memories temporarily erased by said guardian might have humbled her a little, but my aunt stalwartly refused to give up on unearthing the corridor's secrets.

Aunt Candace huffed when she spotted me. "Come to tell me off again?"

"No, I'm here to apologise," I replied. "And to make sure you don't turn yourself into a turnip."

My aunt scoffed. "The riddle says nothing about turnips. There's no danger of that."

"The riddle doesn't mention merging into the wall, either, but you managed that by yourself yesterday."

"Don't be smart with me," she said. "Really, it's quite an ingenious setup on my mother's part. I had to write my desire on the door itself. Of course, with the way that our family's magic works, it seems obvious in retrospect."

"You're planning on writing out all your hopes and dreams onto the door?" I asked. "Until one of them works?"

"One of them *did* work," she said. "What's *your* heart's desire, Rory?"

I blinked. "I'm not writing anything on that door. Besides, my heart's desire..."

My mind went to Laney first and my desire to wake her from sleep, but if I'd been unable to find a solution in the rest of the library, it was unlikely that the fourth-floor corridor would be able to help, either. There was also my driving urge to stop the Founders from harming any more normals, intensified by my experiences today, along with my desire to keep my family safe from their depravities.

"You must have one," Aunt Candace said. "*My* life's ambition is to be a successful enough author that I can move to a distant island and never to have to talk to another person again."

"That's two things, Aunt Candace, and I doubt the door can give you either." If magic was capable of conjuring up money from nowhere, we'd all be millionaires by now. "Have you even done any writing lately?"

"You don't need to lecture me on my own door, Rory."

"Technically, it's Grandma's." I caught sight of a large feathery shape flying over the bookshelves. "Hey… Sylvester."

"What?" The owl landed imperiously on a shelf and peered down at us. "If you're going to ask me to open that door for you, I'd sooner eat it instead."

"What's *your* heart's desire?" Aunt Candace asked, unwisely.

Sylvester let out a sound halfway between a screech and a laugh. "You'd be wise not to ask that question of me again, Candace."

He took flight, wings spread wide, and a huge gust of wind blew at us. I stumbled backward into a shelf, but Aunt Candace remained unruffled. "He's too sensitive."

"Did you forget he's not happy with Grandma for shutting him out of the corridor?" I hissed at her. "Also—he's a genius loci. You'll be lucky if he doesn't trap you in the Dimensional Studies Section for a week."

"You worry too much."

"You don't worry *enough.*"

At the owl's temper tantrum, even the door had turned as white as a sheet.

"Anyway, what was your plan?" I continued. "What if no matter what you write on the door, the room's always full of notebooks you can't read?"

"Enlist my trusty Spell Assistant."

"Right." I had to admire her sheer persistence, if nothing else. "What are you going to do now?"

"Candace?" Aunt Adelaide called from the stairs. "The police just came into possession of a stash of potions, and Edwin has requested your help with identifying them."

"He did what?" I asked blankly. "He asked for Aunt Candace's help? Are you sure?"

Aunt Candace gave a laugh. "Excellent. I knew he'd see my usefulness eventually. I have an extensive list of questions I need to ask him about law enforcement in exchange."

Oh boy.

9

The next morning, I was somewhat prepared for Maura's inevitable appearance, so I went straight to the front desk after breakfast so that I could avoid being startled again. I'd slept a little better, mostly due to sheer exhaustion, but the same couldn't be said of my family members. Aunt Adelaide had had to forcibly drag Aunt Candace out of the police station at the day's end to stop her from spending the night talking Edwin's ear off. I didn't know if she'd managed to find any answers concerning the potions we'd unearthed from the Founders' lab, but I gathered that she'd spent most of the time asking questions about magical criminals instead.

Even though I'd been prepared for Maura to appear, I jumped anyway when she popped out of the shadows next to the front desk. "Are you open yet?"

"No." I jumped again when Xavier followed her lead. "You know, I tend to expect people to knock when they show up out of hours."

"Yes, it's polite," Xavier said sternly. "She insisted on coming here. Sorry, Rory."

"It's not your fault." I swivelled to Maura. "Why so early? Did you find out anything else? About the ghosts and the lab, I mean?"

"No, but your aunt's a real piece of work," Maura said. "I thought that elf policeman was going to fling himself off the pier when she showed up and started badgering him."

"You were at the police station yesterday?"

"They wanted statements from us," Xavier explained. "I managed to talk Edwin out of coming to the library to ask you for a more in-depth statement too."

"Why? I *am* a witness, technically."

"You already gave him the information at the scene," he said. "And the police station was pretty crowded after your aunts showed up."

I hadn't known he'd been there himself, nor Maura either. "Did he give any reason for wanting Aunt Candace's advice?"

"Because she's knowledgeable about potions?" Maura suggested. "I don't know—you're her relation."

"That's why I don't get why he asked her," I replied. "She turned herself into a wall the other day. Listen... what happened to the bodies?"

The two exchanged glances, and Xavier spoke first. "It's not pleasant."

"Please," I said. "Not knowing is worse. What happened?"

"They were... experimented on," Maura said. "They're at the local morgue until the authorities can verify that they aren't going to cause harm to any normal who might touch them."

My stomach churned. "What'll happen to the normals' families? I mean... do they know?"

"Yes, Edwin had his officers call their families and give them an explanation," Xavier said. "He's hoping to return the bodies to them soon."

Shivers sprang to my arms. "I hope he's being careful with those potions. I… I'd like to look at them."

"Why?" Xavier asked.

"Because," I said quietly, "the Founders created those potions themselves, and I don't know if even Edwin's prepared for the possible side effects of handling them."

Understanding sharpened Xavier's gaze. "If you're sure, but I don't think Edwin will have learned anything new since yesterday."

"Nope," Maura said. "Your aunt figured out some of the potions might be deadly poison, but that's as far as she got."

But are any of them possible antidotes? "Wait, does Evangeline know?"

"Good question," Xavier said. "I haven't seen her. You don't want to go there now, do you?"

"Can you imagine what she'll say if she thinks we deliberately kept her in the dark?" I queried. "I bet Edwin didn't tell her."

"If she's a mind reader, she's probably already worked it out," Maura said. "Especially if she's been watching the Founders' house."

"I saw a vampire in the field," I recalled. "Before the ghosts vanished."

"Who?" Xavier asked.

I shook my head. "They moved too fast for me to see their face, and then… we immediately found the lab. I don't know if it was one of Evangeline's people or… or someone else."

"We can tell Edwin," Xavier said. "I'm not sure what he'll do with that information, though. He's already not best pleased about being dragged into the Founders' business again."

"I figured, but I know he'd be ticked off if I'd told Evangeline instead."

"He didn't seem happy with me either," Maura added. "Once he found out I was a Reaper. He kept sighing."

"Oh, he reacts like that to most of us," I said wryly. "I have a tendency to bring trouble to the police on a not-infrequent basis."

"We have that in common," Maura said. "If I wasn't dating the head of our local police force, I'd be in trouble with the authorities more often."

I raised an eyebrow. "You're dating the head of the police? Really?"

"I'll tell you more on the way," she said. "We're going to the police station, right?"

"Sure." I ducked into the living quarters to say goodbye to Aunt Adelaide and Estelle, then the three of us left the library for the seafront.

On the way, Xavier and I managed to wrangle a few details from Maura about her life back in Hawkwood Hollow. Allegedly. she'd walked into the town largely by accident, found it packed full of ghosts, and ended up helping a local family turn their inn into a haunted attraction.

"They're used to me running off at the weekends," she told us. "Since the inn started running ghost tours, Carey and Allie don't have as much time to go ghost hunting them-selves, so I try to scout out locations myself."

"Must be hard when you frighten off most spirits just by looking at them." *Speaking of which...* "Where's your brother?"

She gestured toward the hotel. "He stayed in our room. Said he had too much excitement yesterday."

"He's a ghost. Can they get overstimulated?"

"He's sensitive," she replied. "And he wasn't happy when we found the bodies."

"You didn't seem as bothered," I observed. "I guess you're used to that kind of thing."

"Unfortunately." She crossed the square, slightly ahead of

Xavier and me. "Drew—that's my boyfriend—sees all kinds of unpleasant crap, too, being head of the police. Luckily for him, he can't see ghosts."

"That's why you came alone." I realised that if Maura had been a normal visitor, I might have taken her for a tour of the area, but the rainclouds and the freezing-cold ocean waters didn't exactly make for a holiday mood even without the dour circumstances of her visit.

Maura had already learned her way around, evidently. She strode ahead of us down the street near the clock tower, reached the seafront, and marched straight through the automatic doors into the small police station.

Edwin sighed when he saw us, which came as no surprise. In fairness, I had ruined his weekend by dumping a bunch of dead bodies on him. "Aurora. Let me guess... You want to know what we learned about the bodies that you found. Or are you here to give a more in-depth statement?"

"There's nothing else I can tell you that you don't already know," I replied.

"Except how you knew where to find the hidden building next to that old house?" he enquired. "Nobody else found it, including the other local vampires, I gather."

"I didn't know it was there," I protested. "I spotted the concealment spell when we went looking for ghosts."

"Looking for ghosts," he repeated. "Is that a new hobby of yours?"

His attempt at humour was somewhat undermined by his strained expression. Aunt Candace must have really riled him up, but I hadn't realised the others hadn't mentioned the ghosts to him yet.

"No... they were the ghosts of the Founders' past victims." Admittedly, bringing up the ghosts might raise more questions we couldn't answer, but Edwin himself couldn't see spirits, so he would have to take our word for it.

"Right," he said. "Am I to understand that to put together an explanation that will satisfy the authorities in the town from which the victims were taken, I have to rely on the word of a few ghosts?"

"We spoke to only one of them…" I glanced at Maura and Xavier to back me up. "Someone scared off the ghosts when we found that lab, but we can go back and talk to them again if you need more information. Erm, if we're allowed back in the lab. I know it's probably a crime scene…"

He pinched the bridge of his nose between his fingertips. "I can't stop you from going back, but do you have any idea how hard it is to explain to the regular police force that the bodies were magically tampered with?"

"I can imagine, but isn't it better than the families not knowing at all?" I asked. "Where are the potions you found, anyway?"

"In our back room with the other contraband," he said in brittle tones. "Despite your aunt's efforts to smuggle them back to the library."

Oops. "I can't believe you let Aunt Candace look at them at all. What do you plan to do with them? I assume you aren't keeping them here indefinitely?"

"Once they've been identified, they'll be destroyed," he said. "Frankly, I'd rather destroy them first, but Adelaide insisted otherwise."

Why? Because she thought one might help with the cure for Laney's condition? We hadn't discussed the subject with many people, as I'd also tried to keep her presence in the magical world low-key. She'd been a normal, after all, and though she'd ended up being turned into a vampire, we'd sheltered her in the library before she made the transformation. It was kind of a grey area in magical law, to say the least.

Edwin cleared his throat, evidently expecting an answer.

"Ah… we can take care of them at the library," I offered. "We're used to storing delicate magical objects."

"Or setting them loose in town." He lifted his head as the door slid open behind us, and an expression of resignation came over his face. "Candace."

My aunt bounded into the police station, carrying a briefcase in one hand. "I'm back to help you with those intriguing concoctions."

"What's that?" I asked, indicating the briefcase.

"My collection of alchemical tools."

Had she even been invited to come back today? From the alarm on Edwin's face, I was guessing not, but he gave a sigh and crossed the lobby to unlock an adjacent door.

Aunt Candace practically skipped into the small room, while I approached more slowly, not wanting to get under anyone's feet. The room was occupied by cabinets and shelves and a large table in the centre onto which a number of bottles had been clustered. Some were bright, some dark, and some looked uncomfortably like blood.

"I could have sworn there were more potions than this," Edwin muttered. "Did you sneak one out, Candace?"

"Of course not." She whipped out the briefcase. "Let's see what we have here. Oh… *that's* a memory potion. How intriguing."

Edwin looked like he'd aged several years in the last few minutes as he backed out of the room. "Are none of your other family members experts on potions, Aurora?"

"I don't think so." Aunt Candace was the person in the family who'd spent the longest researching potions to use in her novels. "Not me, anyway."

I looked to Maura, who shrugged. "Yeah, don't look at me. Potions aren't my strong suit."

Xavier wouldn't know, either, which left us at something of a loose end. The room was too small for us all to fit inside, and I wasn't overly keen on supervising my aunt when she might ask *me* to act as a lab rat next. Instead, I awkwardly said goodbye to Edwin and left the police station with the two Reapers.

"Nobody wants Aunt Candace inflicted upon them at this hour of the morning," I remarked to the others. "I thought my Aunt Adelaide only brought her here yesterday so that she'd be too distracted to go to the fourth-floor corridor again."

"What corridor?" Maura asked. "She seems to have extensive knowledge of potions, at least. Out of interest, was there one in particular that you were looking for?"

I'd said too much already, and the desire to unburden myself warred with the urge to keep quiet about Laney.

"A poison that's specifically designed to work on vampires," I hedged. "I know the Founders created at least one, to make sure they could counter any other vampire who betrayed them, and I imagine they'll have had to test them on new vampires to gauge their effectiveness."

"Ouch." Her lips pursed as that sank in. "You wanted to use those same poisons against them?"

"No. I mean, it's kinda hard to poison a vampire when you don't have their speed or other advantages." I returned to the more pertinent subject. "Should we go and see if the ghosts are still around?"

"I gathered that Edwin didn't want anyone going back to the Founders' house," Maura said. "Not that that's the only way to find them."

"Huh?" I looked questioningly at Xavier. "Like what?"

"She can summon the ghosts here," Xavier said disapprovingly. "Through the afterworld."

"You said it, not me," Maura said. "Why not? You didn't actually want to go back to the Founders' house, do you?"

"I don't think the locals want you summoning ghosts in

the middle of town," Xavier commented. "The ghosts won't be a fan either."

"Obviously, I'll pick somewhere that isn't out in public."

"Like your hotel room?" Xavier narrowed his eyes. "Is that appropriate?"

"Why not?" she challenged. "It's far simpler than trying to sneak up on the ghosts without startling them. Unless you want to approach them alone, Rory, and hope that a vampire doesn't appear this time?"

I shivered. No, I didn't want to. "All right, we'll do it this way. If you think the hotel staff won't mind."

"They will," Xavier said. "That said, it's less public than outside. Your brother's still in your room, Maura?"

"Yeah, he won't be thrilled with me for summoning other spirits, but it's not my problem." Maura veered toward the inn. "I can't say the ghosts will answer me, besides. They might have vanished when I found the bodies."

"They might," I said, "but I think we need to speak to Bailey again. She had unfinished business."

If she and the others had been drifting around for weeks, she must have known the lab existed. She would appreciate knowing that her friend Wynn had seemingly escaped unscathed, which might be enough closure, yet a nagging sense that I'd missed something persisted.

The elf at the inn's reception watched us enter, with mild bafflement, but he didn't ask any questions as we walked upstairs to Maura's room. I hoped he hadn't guessed we would be summoning ghosts on the property, but it was that or do so in the library. I doubted my family members would appreciate that, and Sylvester certainly wouldn't.

Maura unlocked her hotel room door. As we followed her into the room, she shooed Mart out of the shower. "This should be pretty straightforward."

"What?" Mart watched Xavier close the door behind us.

"You look like you're going to summon a ghost. You're not going to summon another ghost, are you?"

"Relax, it won't take a minute." Darkness spread from Maura's outstretched hands, wreathing the hotel room, and she spoke. "Bailey?"

Bailey's transparent form appeared amid the darkness, her eyes widening in horror. "What did you do to me?"

"I summoned you," Maura said. "Away from the vampires' house. Thought it might be easier to talk here."

"But where *am* I?"

"Somewhere safer than where you were before," I replied. "You disappeared yesterday. What scared you off?"

She gasped. "You came back to the house? You're the ones who…?"

"Who found your body?"

Bailey whimpered, shrinking back into the darkness. "Please leave me alone. Let me be."

"We're trying to help you." I spoke gently. "You don't want to go back to the house, do you? We can help you move on."

"I just wanted to find Wynn," she whispered.

"We found her," Maura supplied. "She's alive."

Bailey gasped again. "She's alive? Where is she? Is she okay?"

"She's fine." Maura cut through her questions, shadows cloaking her body until she looked more Reaper-like than I'd ever seen her. "I have some questions for you, though."

Bailey flinched. "I don't know anything."

"Maura," I hissed. "Give her space. She's terrified."

"She knows more," she pressed. "You know what the vampires were doing in that lab, don't you, Bailey? You weren't the only person in there."

"No," she whispered. "No, no, no."

"What were they making in that lab?" Maura asked. "What was the end goal?"

Bailey whimpered. "I don't remember. After I got bitten… it's all a blur."

"Did you turn?" Maura asked. "Turn into one of them, I mean? You drank their blood before they bit you, right?"

"I don't know," she whispered. "I remember waking up in the darkness. I couldn't see anything."

"That'd be the lab," Maura surmised. "You'll have slept for a couple of days and woken up pretty groggy, but you must be able to recall some details."

"It was so dark," Bailey said. "There were others there, too. Prisoners."

"Other vampires?" I asked.

"I couldn't see their faces," she whispered. "It was very dark, and I was so *hungry*. I had to drink the… the blood they gave me, though it tasted foul."

"Do you remember when you last saw Wynn?" Maura asked. "Was she a prisoner too?"

"I don't know." She gave another whimper. "I remember telling her to run. I told her to run… I'm glad she survived."

Her voice faded, and so did her ghostly body, becoming one with the darkness.

"She's gone," Xavier said. "I'm pretty sure she moved on. You were right. Wynn was her unfinished business."

"She never told us how Wynn got away from the house." Maura peered at the spot where the ghost had been and let the darkness fade from the room. "Pity we didn't get *her* address."

"Wynn's?" I asked. "Why? She's hardly likely to have been in on the Founders' plan. None of the victims were. They were as scared as she was."

Maura's brow furrowed. "I don't know. Something feels screwy. I can summon one of the other ghosts, but they might not be willing to talk to us."

"Or they moved on." I lifted my head at the sound of

running water from behind the closed bathroom door, but it was only Mart.

"Not again." Maura ran to the bathroom. "Mart, you can't flood the room. I told you."

"Does he make a habit of vandalising hotel rooms?" I asked, curious as to whether the hosts typically knew they had a ghost staying amongst their guests.

"No, he just really likes hot showers." When the water stopped, she turned back to me. "What about this vampire leader of yours, then? Want to speak to her?"

"Maybe," I said. "I bet she's already figured out that we unearthed their hidden lab. She'll have stopped by at Edwin's or sent someone else to snoop around."

"You want to ask if she knows about the potions?" Xavier guessed.

"Edwin said some were missing," I said slowly. "I don't know if he was right, but she's almost certainly figured out what's going on, and she'll be waiting for me to visit. Who knows—she might have some insights."

And so might her mysterious vampire friend.

10

When we neared Evangeline's house, Maura pulled back. "I should wait somewhere Evangeline can't see me. Vampires don't tend to like me."

"I figured." I nodded to Xavier. "Do you want to stay with her?"

His jaw twitched with displeasure. "Sure, but if you need me, I'll be right behind you."

I approached the vampires' home and knocked on the door. I didn't know quite what to expect from Evangeline. She'd almost certainly been plugged into the news of what we'd discovered in the Founders' house, whether anyone had kept her up to date or not. The question was, had she raided Edwin's cupboards, and why?

This time, Evangeline herself answered the door, which surprised me, though maybe it shouldn't have. "Aurora," she said. "What is it?"

"I thought you'd want to know that we found a hidden building near the Founders' house..." I fumbled my words.

"That is, I'm assuming Edwin didn't already tell you what we found in there?"

"Please, get to the point, Aurora," she said. "Your mortal life is too short to waste."

I took a breath. "I expect you've figured some of it out already, but we found the bodies of the Founders' victims, and… and some kind of laboratory."

"Yes, I'm aware of the Founders' unpleasant hobbies," she said. "I confess I didn't expect the location of their experiments to be that close to their house, however."

"Did you know the bodies were hidden inside the lab?" My skin crawled. "They've been there for ages."

"No," she said. "I did not, and even if I had, you can hardly have expected me to contact the human authorities."

I guess not. "I thought you went back to the house, to look for the vampires who escaped."

"Yes," she said. "Briefly, but we did not check the neighbouring fields, and it's going to be impossible to run any further searches now that you've drawn the human authorities' attention."

I blinked at the accusatory note to her voice. "Was I supposed to leave the bodies in there indefinitely? They had families and loved ones who had no idea what happened to them."

I wouldn't expect a vampire to understand the notion of people missing their loved ones, not when she hadn't been alive in centuries, but I couldn't suppress a flicker of irritation at the lack of any comprehension in her expression.

"Anyway," I went on, "we also found a lot of potions in there. Did you know they were experimenting on normals? As well as biting them?"

"Not in that particular instance," she said. "The Founders flaunted the magical laws in numerous ways, but I do not share their depravities."

"But what exactly were they trying to do?" I pressed. "Create new vampires and... what, use them to test their poisons on until they found some that worked?"

"Precisely."

I thought back to Edwin's assertion that some of the potions had gone missing. I didn't have enough of a death wish to outright accuse Evangeline of taking any of them, but if she knew how to identify them by appearance, I would have to ask outright.

"The potions," I said delicately. "Might any of them be... similar to the poison Cateline used?"

A flicker of irritation crossed her face at the mention of the vampire who'd slipped through her clutches by means of her own death. "Not that I've seen so far, but I have an expert examining each of them."

"You have... an expert?" I peered over her shoulder into her house. "In there?"

Evangeline stepped backward in a smooth glide. "If you so desire, you can come inside and assuage your curiosity. I'd prefer not to stand outside in the daylight."

I glanced behind me at Xavier, who stood just out of sight of the door. I figured that I didn't need to provoke Evangeline's ire by reminding her that two Reapers had come with me to her home, so I gave him a nod of reassurance then followed her inside.

The converted church looked much the same as usual, with its dusty stained-glass windows, reams of cobwebs strewn across the ceiling, and the general appearance of somewhere that would be able to host a Halloween party without needing to change the décor in the least.

Without speaking, Evangeline led the way to a narrow staircase that twisted upward in dizzying circles. A door waited at the top, which she opened, revealing a small room occupied by tables and cabinets not unlike those in the

Founders' lab. An array of bottles and jars sat upon the wooden tables, along with vials and bowls and other alchemical paraphernalia.

"Did you take *all* of those from the police station behind Edwin's back?" I couldn't help asking her.

A laugh answered, and Victoire stepped out from behind a cabinet. "Aurora, what a nice surprise. You invited her here to see the lab, did you, Evangeline?"

I tensed, not liking the knowing glint in her eyes. "This is *your* lab?"

"A temporary one." She laughed again. "Yes, I dabbled in alchemy both during life and in death, so I decided to step in to help identify some of these fascinating concoctions."

"You used to be a witch, then?" I guessed. "Before you turned into a vampire?"

"A very long time ago," she said with a pointy-toothed smile. "But I find that I only truly came into my talents after leaving the mortal realm behind."

Evangeline made a noise halfway between a growl and a hiss. "You overstep, Victoire. I told you not to toy with the humans, including those foolish enough to show up on my doorstep."

Thanks for that. "Actually, I am interested to know about your lab," I said to Victoire. "Have you identified any of those potions Evangeline gave you?"

"Oh, I like this one." She laughed. "Don't be so dour, Evangeline. She's curious, and that is a trait I am always keen to reward. You see, Aurora, I used to be Carlos Verdant's apprentice, many centuries ago."

My mouth parted. *She was his apprentice?* Yet Evangeline had invited her into her home? "You worked for *him?*"

"Oh, don't look so scandalised," she said. "Things were different in those days, and the Founders were the forerunners of knowledge and discovery. Even Evangeline respected them, didn't you?" she added to the vampires' leader.

I gaped at Evangeline, but she ignored me, instead regarding Victoire. "*Have* you identified any of those potions?"

"Have a little patience," said Victoire. "Some are undoubtedly enhancers, but most are new to me."

I studied the collection of bottles. "What do you mean by 'enhancers'?"

"Potions that give vampires enhanced abilities." Victoire smiled. "We already have superior speed and strength and an endless lifespan, but with the right mixture of ingredients, it's possible for us to far surpass humanity. We can even compensate for certain, ah, weaknesses… or on the contrary, we can exploit those weaknesses in others."

Is she telling the truth? It was plain to see that even Evangeline didn't trust her, but Victoire clearly knew what she was talking about. While Victoire had some serious nerve playing mind games with the vampires' leader, Evangeline must have had faith in her knowledge if she trusted the other vampire with a room inside her home to conduct her experiments.

"By weaknesses," I said, "do you mean some of the potions are designed to kill other vampires?"

"Possibly," she replied. "However, it's somewhat hard to run certain tests without a willing subject."

My heart lurched at the reminder of Laney. "You can't expect any of the vampires to volunteer as lab rats. There's a reason the Founders had to break the law and kidnap normals instead."

"Yes… I understand why they felt the need to do so," she said. "Imagine the discoveries that would be made if people were more open-minded. I'd certainly make progress far quicker if someone were to step forward…" She gestured invitingly, reaching out to touch my face, and I took a step backward.

Okay, she's officially creeping me out.

"That is quite enough," Evangeline said in sharp tones. "I gave you access to those potions on the condition that you do *not* test them on anyone in this community, vampire or otherwise. If you cannot respect my conditions, I'll have to ask you to leave my property."

"You mistake me." Victoire lowered her hand. "I was merely curious as to this little mortal's interest in my lab. Most humans are woefully closed-minded."

"I'm not interested in being a lab rat." I had to make that clear, at least. "Nobody else in Ivory Beach is either."

"Precisely." Evangeline beckoned. "Let us leave her to her experiments, Aurora."

I didn't want to spend another minute in the same room as Victoire, and I gladly turned away from her laughing face.

When we reached the foot of the stairs, I asked Evangeline the question that had been burning inside my head since we'd entered the lab. "She used to be his apprentice," I whispered. "Carlos Verdant. Why invite her into your home?"

"Because she knows him and his ilk," she said. "He might have fled his home, but her knowledge will enable me to track him down."

"I didn't know Carlos Verdant escaped." A shiver sprang to my skin. "I thought you killed him. Or jailed him."

Her mouth showed a fanged smile. "If he has any sense, he'll have fled the country, but if not, I look forward to the day that we next meet face-to-face."

Now she's creeping me out too. At least Evangeline had a moral compass, even if it occasionally pointed in the wrong direction. "Do you think there's a chance any of those potions might be... I mean, did Carlos Verdant and his allies help develop the poison that was used on Laney?"

"At this point, I cannot say," she said, "but I'd advise you not to give that particular piece of information to Victoire."

"She might have already read my thoughts." She had no boundaries, as was abundantly clear, and I'd been too freaked out earlier to ensure I was guarding my innermost secrets. Yet I was struggling to see a way to resolve Laney's situation without the aid of an expert in the poison she'd been afflicted with.

"She might," Evangeline said, "which is why I would advise you to stay away from my home until she has departed. I shall bring you any news that might emerge in the meantime."

Her tone suggested that she doubted Victoire would be able to help, but I had zero desire to go back upstairs and ask more questions. Instead, I took Evangeline's suggestion and left the vampires' house.

Xavier met me outside. "Maura's gone to the library," he told me. "Are you all right?"

I nodded. "Yeah, just mildly creeped out. That friend of Evangeline's—you know, the one we met the other day—she used to be Carlos Verdant's apprentice."

Shock widened his eyes. "She let him into her home?"

"Not only that, but Victoire's set up a lab upstairs and is lamenting the lack of human volunteers to experiment on."

"That's... disturbing."

"I know, right?" I slid my hand into his as we walked away from the vampires' home. "She's helping Evangeline identify the potions from the lab because she's supposedly an alchemy expert, but I don't trust her an inch."

"I expect Evangeline knows what she's doing," he said. "She wouldn't have invited a potential enemy into her home unless she was certain she could keep her under control."

"You'd think." I grimaced. "Wait, did you say Maura went to the library?"

He inclined his head. "I know I'm supposed to keep an eye on her, but I didn't want to leave you alone here."

"I guess Maura isn't the least trustworthy recent visitor in town," I remarked. "Has your boss brought her up at all?"

"No, he didn't even ask me any questions about her yesterday," he said. "He did ask me about the lab, but only to verify that the ghosts disappeared once we discovered their bodies."

"Did they, though?" It wasn't like the Grim Reaper not to be thorough about such matters. "That reminds me—I forgot to ask Victoire how she ended up being acquainted with your boss."

"I doubt she'd have told you," he said. "My boss certainly won't, but her presence in town might explain why he's been in such a mood."

"Is he ever *not* in a foul mood?"

I ducked into the bakery to buy lunch then crossed the square back to the library.

When we entered, we found Maura near the front desk, talking to Aunt Candace, of all people. *Oh boy.*

"Hey." Maura eyed my bag of sandwiches with considerable interest. "Can I have one of those?"

"Sure, go ahead." I was glad I'd bought some spares, especially when Aunt Candace swiped a sandwich for herself without asking. "Aunt Candace, I thought you were at the police station."

"Edwin kicked her out." Maura took a bite of her sandwich.

"He didn't, did he?" I swivelled to Aunt Candace. "What did you do?"

Aunt Candace huffed. "He's just being sensitive. I offered to taste some of the potions myself, and he acted as if I'd threatened to murder him."

"You offered to do *what?*" It was a good job *she* hadn't

been in the vampires' home when Victoire had declared her search for potential lab rats. "Most of the potions are designed for vampires, not humans."

"That's inconvenient," Aunt Candace said.

"If you say so." I finished my sandwich then turned to Maura. "What do you want to do now? Check to see if the other ghosts also disappeared?"

Maura crumpled her sandwich wrapper in her hand. "What about Bailey's friend? The one who survived."

"Wynn." Come to think of it, I did have a few questions I wanted to ask her. "She's a living witness, but I don't know that we can count on finding her outside Bailey's house again."

"Reaper, remember?" Maura said. "I can track her. Xavier can too."

"All right." I faced my aunt. "Aunt Candace, you stay here. Where are Estelle and Aunt Adelaide?"

"Decorating." She pursed her lips. "Apparently, they needed to repaint the third floor."

Most likely, they'd wanted to keep her away from the fourth-floor corridor so she didn't get up to any more mischief after Edwin kicked her out of the police station.

"All right." I turned back to the others. "Xavier, you can find Wynn from here, right?"

"Yes, but I can't actually see her location," he replied. "I don't want to materialise in front of a bunch of normals."

"Definitely not." Maura stepped toward the door. "We can start at Bailey's house and go from there."

"Good call." I opted to use a transportation spell this time and got out my wand. "See you there."

I pictured the street where Bailey's house was located. In a wave of my wand, the library was replaced by the row of terraced houses, and Maura and Xavier followed a moment later.

"I can't sense her," Maura said. "Isn't she local?"

"Yes." Xavier's forehead crinkled. "I can't find her, either."

"Weird." I scanned the houses, my gaze landing on the bushes surrounding Bailey's front garden, and a flicker of movement caught my eye. "Wait."

I hurried in that direction. When she saw us, Wynn blanched. "You again?"

"Why can't we sense you, I wonder?" Maura said. "Let's see."

She vanished into shadow and reappeared behind Wynn, who jumped a foot in the air, literally.

"I knew it." Maura wore an expression of triumph on her face. "You're one of them."

Wynn ran, far faster than any human could move, vanishing around the corner. I broke into a sprint, not wanting to lose sight of her. "Wait!"

Wynn skidded to a halt when Maura reappeared in front of her. *A vampire. She's a vampire.* From her wide eyes and evident terror, she barely had a grasp on her new reality, and her panic intensified when Xavier approached from behind and cut off her only route of escape.

Seeing that there was no way out, Wynn burst into tears. "Let me go!"

"Please don't," Maura said. "I don't want to have to drag you through the afterworld to stop you from screaming the place down and alerting the normals."

"Maura," I warned. "You're scaring her half to death."

"She's *already* dead," Maura retaliated. "Which is a problem. She shouldn't be around normals."

"I don't understand what you want from me," Wynn whimpered between sobs. "Bailey's dead. Her parents know, and so does everyone else."

"She was looking for you," I told her. "At the house. You were there, weren't you? You were bitten too?"

Her eyes filled with tears. "I... I didn't know they *killed* her. How do you know all this?"

"She's a ghost," Maura supplied. "We spoke to her."

"A ghost?" Wynn shook her head. "You're lying."

"Is that any less likely than a vampire?" Maura said, though not unkindly. "Bailey's been haunting the house for weeks because she thought *you* were there. I assume you escaped, didn't you? You ran back home, high on vampire blood, and fell into a coma."

Wynn began sobbing again. "A ghost. *A ghost.* Why did she die and not me?"

"We'd like to know that too," I said. "If you tell us what you know..."

Wynn sniffed. "I don't know anything."

"You were at the party," I said. "What happened? Do you remember being bitten?"

"No," she said. "At the party, they... I think I was drugged. That whole night is a blur."

"They might have given her a memory potion," Maura muttered. "Didn't your aunt recognise one of them at the police station?"

"True." Although those potions would be an easier way for the vampires to ensure that normals didn't recall the experience, I wasn't convinced that Wynn had given us the full picture. "Wynn, do you remember being taken somewhere else? Somewhere outside the house?"

"No..." She trailed off. "I remember leaving the party. I thought they must have drugged the wine because I moved so fast it was like I was flying. And I remember my dad was furious with me for coming back home late. We argued, I think... and then I passed out in bed."

"And didn't wake up for three days," Maura guessed.

She winced. "I thought I had the flu. I was so *tired,* and everything tasted weird."

"Except human blood?" Maura pressed. "I'm guessing you figured it out eventually, and you can't be telling me you kept it all a secret from every person in your life."

"Does anyone else know?" I asked. She wasn't like Laney—she didn't have a friend willing to induct her into the magical world. "Like your parents?"

"No," she said. "They're divorced. I see my mum only a couple of times a year, and my dad's too busy with my younger siblings to notice. He grounded me after the party, but only for, like, a week. He knew I was worried about Bailey, and he wasn't going to stop me from hanging around at her house."

I guess not. What were we supposed to do with her, though? Call Evangeline? Given my own experience, the library wasn't the worst place to start, as far as magical inductions went, but meeting Aunt Candace wouldn't do anything to ease her apprehension about all things magical.

"We can help you," I offered. "If you come with us."

"Will you let me talk to Bailey?" Wynn asked. "I just want to say sorry."

I shook my head. "Sorry. Even most people like us can't see ghosts, and I'm not sure she's still around."

She opened her mouth to reply, then her eyes widened with fear. Without a word, she bolted, darting past Xavier faster than a flash of light. I swivelled to see what had frightened her so badly and saw Victoire had appeared at the end of the street.

"Fancy meeting you here, Aurora." She smiled at us. "What's all this?"

"What do you mean, what's all this?" I asked. "Why are you here? This is a normal town."

"Is it?" She eyed the row of brick houses. "How quaint."

"Were you *following* me?" Tension gripped my shoulders. "I thought you were at Evangeline's house. In the lab."

"I hit something of a roadblock, as you mortals say," Victoire said. "I decided to get some air."

"Why here?" Xavier's eyes narrowed at her. "Did you know there was a new vampire running around amongst normals?"

Now that Wynn had run off, I hadn't a hope of finding her again, not with her newly enhanced vampire speed.

In response, Victoire smiled again. "Would you prefer to bring the little normal to Evangeline and to take her away from her family and friends?"

"You *did* know?" My hands clenched. "What *are* you doing here?"

"Sightseeing." And she was gone, leaving a dozen more questions drifting in her wake.

11

We scoured the area, looking for Wynn, but Xavier and Maura's Reaper abilities didn't allow them to track vampires, not even newly made ones who'd been mortal not so long ago. In the end, I reluctantly decided that Evangeline was better equipped to find the missing newly created vampire than the rest of us were. She would certainly want to know that Victoire had been aware and had decided to keep Wynn's location from the vampires' leader.

Maura, Xavier, and I discussed the possibilities at length, debating whether Victoire was actively working with the Founders or just trying to make trouble all on her own. Either might be possible, but when we arrived back in Ivory Beach, I decided to go to the vampires' home again.

"While you're there, I'm going to look for the other ghosts," Maura said.

"Are you, now?" Xavier asked. "Can I trust you to come back and tell us if you find them?"

"Sure," she said. "Does your boss even care what I do?"

Xavier's mouth flattened. "If we aren't at Evangeline's place, you can find us at the library."

"Would *he* want to know Victoire is running around, making trouble?" I figured not, given the Grim Reaper's general lack of interest in anything not related to the Reapers, but a new vampire was a potential threat to the secrecy of the magical world at large.

"My boss hasn't mentioned her either," Xavier said as Maura vanished into the shadows. "He might not be happy that I'm letting Maura run around unsupervised, so I'll avoid going back home until she's back."

"Good idea."

I approached the vampires' home and knocked on the door, but this time, nobody answered.

"She might have gone back to bed since it's daytime," Xavier said. "Or she's out looking for Victoire herself."

"Maybe." *We'll have to come back later.* "Let's make sure Aunt Candace hasn't gone back to the police station again."

We entered the library to the sound of an owl's cry from somewhere upstairs. Estelle, who was in the process of tidying a stack of returns, jumped in surprise. "What—oh, hey, Rory."

"Did I just hear Sylvester?"

"Yes, but I don't know what Aunt Candace did this time." She looked past me. "Hey, Xavier. Where's the other Reaper?"

"She's gone to talk to ghosts." I drew in a breath. "There's been a new development. It turns out Bailey's friend Wynn escaped the Founders because they turned her into a vampire."

"Oh no." She sucked in a breath. "Is she still living with the normals?"

"Yes, and thanks to Evangeline's 'friend,' she's taken off, and we have no idea where she is," I said distractedly.

"Where's Aunt Candace? I thought you banned her from the fourth floor."

"We had to let her back up there eventually," Estelle said. "It was that or let her go and pester Edwin. She promised not to turn herself into a wall again."

"Sounds like she's aggravating Sylvester instead." I rubbed my forehead. "You won't believe the morning we've had."

I filled her in and Aunt Adelaide, too, when she showed up halfway through my explanation.

"I think your best option is to ask Evangeline to deal with that new vampire," Aunt Adelaide said when I'd finished. "The poor girl. It's an awful situation."

"Yeah, Evangeline isn't likely to let her down gently," I said. "I don't know where Evangeline is now, but that friend of hers..."

Another screech from upstairs made us all jump.

"What *is* that owl doing?" Aunt Adelaide lifted her head. "I told my sister *not* to write anything else on that door, but maybe she's trying to convince Sylvester to help instead."

"That'll end well." I turned to Xavier. "Want to check up on her?"

"All right," he said dubiously. "I suppose after Victoire, dealing with Aunt Candace won't be too much bother."

"Don't speak too soon." I got out my Biblio-Witch Inventory as we climbed the stairs, just in case.

When we reached the third floor, I spotted the owl perched on a bookshelf, peering down at Aunt Candace. My aunt stood in front of the entrance to the fourth-floor corridor, holding what appeared to be a pen and wearing the expression of someone who'd found a hoard of solid gold.

"What's going on?" I asked. "Is that... a pen?"

Sylvester emitted another loud screech, drowning out her reply.

I covered my ears. "What's the problem? That pen isn't a bomb in disguise, is it?"

"Of course not," Aunt Candace said. "I lost my pen, so I asked the room to find it for me, and here it is."

"Huh?" I studied the pen, which looked pretty ordinary to me. "You opened the door?"

"Yes, I opened the door, and the pen was lying on the floor." She spun it between her fingers. "See?"

"No mishaps involving walls this time?" I asked. "What else was in the room?"

"Nothing, of course," she said. "I asked for the pen, and the room provided."

"The room granted your wish?" Xavier asked in surprise.

"You can't try it out, Reaper," she said. "It's for family members only."

"No… you have to write on the door, right?" My mind spun with the possibilities. "That was your heart's desire? To find your missing pen?"

"At that particular moment in time." She grinned. "I'll never lose anything again."

"I wouldn't go that far," I said. "I mean, if it's like the Forbidden Room, it'll only be able to affect things in the library."

Sylvester let out a deafening screech and took flight with a gale-force wind, knocking me clean off my feet. Aunt Candace staggered back, and even Xavier stumbled a little.

"Rory, are you okay?" he asked.

"Yeah." I lifted my head. "I shouldn't have said that. It *does* sound similar, though." That made sense, as Grandma was the one who'd created the Book of Questions *and* the Forbidden Room in the first place.

"Oh, he doesn't like that room a bit," Aunt Candace said with a laugh. "It might even be able to do *more* than that book of his. I've always wanted to go to space. Or another dimension."

"We don't have time to rescue you from another dimension, Aunt Candace." I sat upright and pushed to my feet. "Be careful. If the room is interpreting everything you say literally, it's no wonder you turned into a wall."

"Oh, don't worry," she said. "I learned my lesson from that one. But think of the possibilities!"

"I bet it can't get rid of the Founders… No, don't ask for that," I said hastily as she moved into the doorway. "Not until we know the limits."

"Why not?" she asked. "The room can solve all our problems."

"And create new ones, no doubt." I folded my arms. "Look, there's got to be some level of restriction on what you can ask for. The corridor can't affect anything outside the library."

"That doesn't matter." Her eyes lit up. "I bet it can give us a weapon to destroy them."

"What, like the poison—wait, don't ask for that either," I said hastily. "You have the recipe, and you could have brewed some yourself if you hadn't been up here instead. Besides, it's the antidote we need."

The antidote. The word rang in my skull, and a possibility bloomed to life in my chest. Was the antidote for Laney's condition on the other side of that door? No way. It couldn't be that simple.

"Would you like to try?" she asked. "Just write your heart's desire onto the door, and the room shall provide."

What is my heart's desire?

My chest tightened. *To save Laney. To stop the Founders.* But Grandma hadn't had to worry about them, had she? She'd known they existed, no doubt, but I'd thought my dad had been the first person in the family to draw their ire.

"What?" Aunt Candace asked. "What's with that look?"

"Nothing." The hope felt too fragile, as though it might be snuffed out if I examined it too closely. "I think you should talk to the others before you try asking for anything else. That room is powerful and dangerous."

She gave an exaggerated sigh. "You're old before your time, Rory, but I shall oblige."

My aunt peeled herself away from the doorway and followed Xavier and me to the stairs. I hadn't taken a step before the stairs collapsed and became a slide. I tumbled downward, head over heels, and caught my balance as something transparent and sticky came flying down from above and landed on my head.

"Sylvester!" The stuff was even in my *hair*. "What—Is this glue?"

"Looks like a spiderweb," Aunt Candace came sliding down to join me. "Not to worry."

She made the sticky web vanish with a wave of her wand, and Xavier caught up a moment later. "Rory, you're not hurt, are you?"

"I'm fine, but I think Sylvester is jealous of the room." I dropped my voice in case the owl was still listening in. "Which is ridiculous because they can do exactly the same."

I figured Sylvester was having a hard time not being the foundation of all information in the library, but I was having an equally hard time sympathising by the time the third web landed on my head on my way downstairs.

We found Estelle waiting for us in the lobby. "What in the world did you do to Sylvester?"

"Aunt Candace figured out how to control the room up on the fourth floor," I explained. "She asked it to find her missing pen, and it worked, so Sylvester had a fit of jealousy."

"Whoa," Estelle said. "Are you sure she didn't just put the pen into the room herself?"

"Are you accusing me of deceit?" Aunt Candace seized her niece's arm and made to pull her toward the stairs. "I'll prove it to you."

"I don't want Sylvester to throw more Halloween decorations at me," Estelle protested. "He's already destroyed half my artificial spiderwebs."

"I wondered where those came from." I moved in front of Aunt Candace. "Come on—let go of her."

"What *are* you doing?" Aunt Adelaide came over to us. "Are you the reason it's raining spiderwebs, Candace?"

Aunt Candace released Estelle and made a placating gesture. "Our dear owl is having a slight existential crisis."

"He's in a sulk because Aunt Candace figured out how to use the room to get whatever she wants," I explained. "I think it adapts, depending on what you ask for—exactly like the Book of Questions."

"What?" Her eyes grew wide. "Another Forbidden Room? Our mother made *two* of them?"

"Isn't it wonderful?" Aunt Candace beamed. "Instead of asking your question to a capricious owl, you simply write it onto the door."

"Which means it'll only work for our family members," Estelle surmised. "If Grandma made two, it's no wonder she locked one of them away. Can you use the room more than once per day?"

"That's a good point." I swivelled to Aunt Candace. "Did you try any other wishes before that one?"

"I did not," she said. "But it doesn't matter if I can only use it once per day, does it?"

"No, but it's dangerous," Aunt Adelaide said. "In the wrong hands, at least. Nobody is to speak a word of this outside of the library."

Tension laced her words, and I nodded. "Of course. Xavier won't either, right…?"

I trailed off, realising Xavier had vanished. A scan of the lobby showed that someone else had materialised near the desk and that he'd gone to meet them. Maura was back.

I ran to catch up to them. "That was fast. How long have you been standing there?"

"Something weird is going on," she said. "The ghosts have vanished. All of them."

"Really?" I frowned.

"I tried summoning each of them, and nobody replied," she said. "I went to look around the field, and it's empty. So is the house."

Had someone used a banishing spell, or had the ghosts all vanished when their bodies had been discovered, like I'd thought?

"Weird. I guess they moved on," I said.

"Have you spoken to Evangeline?" Maura asked.

"She didn't answer the door," I said. "I thought she might have gone after Victoire, but we can head back and see if she's around."

As curious as I might have been about the implications of Aunt Candace solving the puzzle of the upstairs room, I was happy to get away from the crackling tension amongst my family members.

Once again, I left the library with the two Reapers. I spared a glance for the cemetery on the way uphill, but no signs of the Grim Reaper materialised. Did *he* know of the newly created vampire? Surely not.

At the vampires' house, we found Evangeline waiting outside, her expression perturbed. "Aurora, what is it now?"

"We found Wynn—the friend of one of the Founders' victims—and she'd been turned into a vampire," I said in a rush. "I came here to tell you before, but you weren't in."

Her eyes narrowed. "You left this other vampire behind?"

"Your friend Victoire appeared and frightened her off,

and we didn't have a hope of catching up to a vampire running away at top speed."

"Not even with two Reapers accompanying you?" she enquired, her gaze momentarily drifting toward where Xavier and Maura waited a few feet away.

"They weren't familiar with the area, and they can't track vampires," I explained. "I don't know what Victoire was playing at, but it seems suspicious to me that she was hanging around a town where normals live. I don't think she's being honest with you."

"Don't you, Aurora?"

When would I learn that talking about a vampire behind their back would always end badly? I cringed inwardly as I turned to see Victoire herself approaching us, her pointed teeth bared in her customary smile.

"There you are," Evangeline said. "Is it true?"

"Is what true?" Victoire's face was the picture of innocence. "That I am scheming against you? Did you not send me to find the Founders' current hideout yourself?"

"You did?" I swivelled back to Evangeline. "I... I didn't know you sent her to find the Founders' hideout. Or that there was another one at all."

Evangeline scowled. "Victoire was proving somewhat *restless,* so I asked her to check up on some old contacts. I didn't know she planned to ambush a newly created vampire and scare her off."

"That's an unnecessarily accusatory tone, especially as I've put all this effort into finding Carlos Verdant's current location," Victoire remarked. "And I was successful, in fact."

"You were?" Evangeline narrowed her eyes. "Tell me more at once."

"Dear Carlos moved back into his old house," Victoire said. "You can read my mind if you don't believe me."

What? I didn't trust her a bit, but she'd been apprenticed to Carlos Verdant. *And if anyone would know where he was hiding...*

Her smile broadened. "I do hope you're ready to apologise, Aurora."

My shoulders tensed when her attention locked on me, but to my surprise, it was Evangeline who stepped in. "What do you expect? You scared off that vampire for no reason at all."

"I expect she'll show up again soon." Victoire laughed. "Unless Carlos takes her in."

Dread rushed down my spine. "Is that likely?"

"It wouldn't be the first time." A smile played on her lips. "You want the address? It's Twelve Welling Street... but you'll have a hard job getting inside without drawing attention."

"Why would he hide somewhere that obvious?" I asked. "I mean, if he lived there before, he must have known it'd be one of the first places you'd look."

"Carlos didn't expect *me* to turn on him," she said. "It's hard for us to disobey the one who sired us."

The word brought a flicker of recognition. *Sire... the person who'd created her.*

"You managed it, though," I said. "Whereabouts is this house? Not in the middle of nowhere, I assume?"

"I'd like to know the same." Evangeline glared at her. "Well?"

"Kingshill," Victoire said. "Its proximity to normals makes it difficult to break into with magical means, as you can imagine."

"What? It's near where we met you?" Dread gripped me. *Near where Laney was recruited. And Wynn, and Bailey...* It made an awful kind of sense that Carlos Verdant's other base was near the place where he'd recruited hapless normals. He wouldn't have had to look far to find possible targets.

"Precisely," Victoire said. "Do you not want to punish

Carlos Verdant for defying you, Evangeline? And you, Aurora... do you not want to obtain the antidote to your friend's condition?"

"What?" A mixture of anger and shock assailed me. "Stop reading my thoughts."

"Oh, Aurora, your tragedy breaks my heart," she said. "How could I ignore your pain?"

"That is enough," Evangeline growled. "Come in, and tell me everything you know, and I'll decide whether to believe you."

"All right." Victoire caught my eye. "If you want to come with me, meet me outside in an hour."

Evangeline's scowl was intense enough that I didn't quite dare answer. While I was still reeling, Victoire vanished into the church, and the door closed behind her.

Xavier, who'd been watching, crossed the path to embrace me. "What did she say to you?"

"I..." I faltered when Maura caught up to us, eyeing the vampires' home.

"Any luck this time?" she asked.

"Yes... and no," I said. "Victoire claimed to be searching for the Founders' hideout when we ran into her. She claims she was successful at finding Carlos Verdant's location and even gave Evangeline the address."

"You trust her word?" Maura asked.

"Of course I don't." I shook my head. "But we don't have any other leads, and she let Evangeline glimpse her thoughts to prove she was telling the truth."

"I wouldn't take the risk," Xavier said. "She clearly has no qualms about deceiving the other vampires, including Evangeline."

"There's an easy way to check," Maura said. "I can get up close to the address without running the risk of walking into any traps. So can your boyfriend."

True, but the ease with which she'd revealed Carlos Verdant's location felt like a trap in itself. "Evangeline might want to go there alone."

"Would she want to dirty her hands?" Maura queried. "From what you've told me, she's not the sort."

No... but what if Carlos Verdant has the cure for Laney?

And what if he's still capturing normals to experiment on too?

12

For lack of any better options, the three of us returned to the library to discuss what to do next. My family members reacted exactly as I expected to the newest bombshell that the vampires had dropped on our heads.

"Don't trust her," Estelle warned. "That Victoire has her own agenda. Who's to say she ever *stopped* working for the Founders?"

"The thought crossed my mind too," I admitted, "but if this is some elaborate trap, Evangeline isn't going to be easily fooled. Besides, if the Founders have been hiding among normals all this time..."

"Leave it to Evangeline," said Aunt Adelaide firmly. "Isn't she supposed to be responsible for handling these situations?"

"Yes, but if Victoire is right, the Founders' safe house is too close to normals for anyone to risk causing too much of a stir," I explained. "Also... Carlos Verdant is there."

"Him?" Estelle shuddered. "He's the one who was doing those creepy experiments, is he?"

"Exactly," I said. "Also, there's a newly turned vampire on the loose, and I bet those creeps would love to recapture her."

"If my Reaper abilities let me track vampires, I'd go looking for her again," Maura added. "But I have no idea where to find her. She won't have gone back to her friend's house again, will she?"

"I don't know." Unease skittered down my spine. "I'd also like to know how close her house is to the Founders' hideout. Since we ran into Victoire there…"

"I know." Xavier's brow pinched. "I'd say it's likely to be close. It's also likely that Victoire will go after Wynn again, given the chance."

"And what, recruit her?" Maura asked. "I don't know, Evangeline might put her foot down first."

"Unless Evangeline's more interested in chasing down Carlos Verdant." *Assuming he hadn't already got wind of her approach.* "We have an hour to make a decision, either way."

"Rory…" Estelle paused. "I don't like the timing of this. Wasn't that Victoire supposed to be helping identify the potions you found in the lab? Why'd she suddenly decide to go hunting the Founders?"

"I think that's why she was originally here," I explained. "Evangeline knew of her past connection with the Founders."

"Meaning she worked for Carlos Verdant," Aunt Adelaide said. "I don't like the timing either. If Verdant *is* where Victoire says he is, he'll almost certainly know that you unearthed his secret lab. If you then deliver yourself into his hands…"

"That's not the plan," I said. "Xavier… Well, it's up to him, but a Reaper can easily get in and out of any safe house without the vampires being any the wiser. Unless you think your boss would object?" I added to Xavier.

"Yes, he would, but that's never stopped me before," he

said. "Also, Maura doesn't have that restriction. Assuming *she* wants to check out the house."

Maura gave a shrug. "Not much else I can do now the ghosts have gone."

"What, all of them?" Estelle asked.

"Yeah," I replied. "I guess once we found their bodies, their unfinished business was dealt with, but... I don't know."

"I can look," Xavier offered. "I might as well do something that doesn't involve going back to the cemetery and potentially alerting the boss of Victoire's invitation."

"Ah." I didn't want to land him in trouble with the Grim Reaper. Though it struck me that Xavier's boss might have been aware of the Founders' new hiding place, too, it wasn't worth drawing his ire, not when I needed a Reaper's help to get into the Founders' hideout—and to find out if a cure for Laney's condition was hidden inside.

Rationally, I knew the odds were stacked against me, but I wouldn't have many opportunities to face the Founders in a scenario where they were decidedly at a disadvantage. No matter how many allies Carlos Verdant might have in his new hideout, he would have a hard time evading two Reapers *and* Evangeline's fellow vampires even if Victoire took his side in the end.

"See you soon." Xavier gave me a brief kiss. "I won't be long."

He vanished, and a heartbeat later, Maura did the same.

"Guess she didn't want to wait around." I assumed she was going back to her hotel room to check up on her brother. "Did you ever find any books that might help her?"

"No," Estelle responded. "Which makes me wonder what's in it for her. Why would she risk her safety by storming a vampire's hideout?"

"Most Reapers don't view risks in quite the same way as

the rest of us do," I reminded her. "It's probably a standard weekend for her."

"Typical." Estelle shook her head. "Why anyone would *choose* to go chasing after that Carlos Verdant… I didn't even know he was still at large. I thought he was in prison."

"Who's in prison?" Cass approached us from behind. "Not Aunt Candace, I hope."

"No, she's working on a book," Aunt Adelaide said. "I managed to convince her to write notes on her discovery, to keep her from going back to pester Edwin."

"I did wonder where she'd gone." I swivelled toward Cass. "What have you been doing all day?"

"*Not* chasing vampires, testing dodgy potions, or turning myself into furniture," she replied, somewhat cryptically. "What did you do to Sylvester? He's been hiding in my room all afternoon. I had to lure him out from under my bed with a dead mouse."

"He has?" Had she been taking care of him? That was unexpectedly heartfelt of her, though maybe not so unexpected, given her recent devotion to watching Laney. "Do I want to know why you had a dead mouse?"

"For the manticore, of course."

"Right." I shook my head. "Well, you might want to sit down. It's been a day."

Explaining the events of that day took the better part of an hour. At least it was a welcome distraction from my worries concerning the Founders and their allies.

"Let me get this straight," Cass said. "You trust the word of a vampire who used to be a *Founder*? And Evangeline does too?"

"Of course I don't trust her," I replied. "But if the Founders are still in the region, I don't really blame Evangeline for wanting to hunt them down. Not to mention a rogue vampire living amongst normals is a danger to everyone, including herself."

"Leave them to it," Cass said. "The vampires can finish each other off for all I care."

"I'm not planning on wading into the middle of their fight," I clarified, "but Wynn's an innocent bystander—a normal, like Laney was."

Anger flickered in her eyes, then she whipped out her wand as Maura appeared next to the desk.

"Whoa," Maura said. "It's just me. We have a problem."

"There is no 'we,'" Cass said. "What, did the vampires chase you off?"

"Not exactly." She held up a folded piece of paper. "I found this inside the lab."

"At Ridgeway House?" I peered at the paper, and my blood went cold.

The note said simply, "Thank you for returning my escaped lab rat."

"I think I know who the note is referring to," Maura added. "Xavier thought so too, but he was going to check Bailey's house in case it was a false alarm."

"And if not?" *If not... the Founders have taken Wynn.* "Why leave the note in the lab?"

"Obviously, someone has been following you around," Cass said impatiently. "Someone who conveniently invited you to infiltrate the Founders' base with her."

"I don't know if she left the note," I said. "She knows we have two Reapers on our side. Carlos Verdant might not, and Xavier and Maura can run circles around them both."

"Gladly," Maura added. "We can hop in and out of the Founders' house and rescue Wynn without any trouble."

With two Reapers on our side, the vampires would have a hard time cornering us, but something about the obvious nature of Victoire's duplicity made me uneasy. Would it really be that simple?

Aunt Adelaide sucked in a breath. "I'm not going to lecture you on what risks to take, Maura, but Rory…"

"I'm not going into the Founders' house until Carlos Verdant and his allies are out of it," I said. "I just want to make sure Wynn is safe."

At that moment, the library door flew open, and a towering shadow fell upon all of us. The Grim Reaper loomed in the doorway, a fearsome figure blocking out all the remaining daylight.

"Where is my apprentice, Aurora?" he boomed.

"Erm… he's around." I tried to catch Maura's eye, but even she looked startled at the Grim Reaper's transformation into a giant.

"You sent him away on an absurd errand, didn't you?"

"He chose to go himself," I said. "He'll be back soon."

Why now? It'd been such a long time since I'd ticked off the Grim Reaper that I'd forgotten how terrifying he could be, but he couldn't have picked a worse time to put his shadowy foot down. Even Maura looked mildly cowed, while my family members had gone silent, even Cass.

"I've made allowances for you, Aurora, but sending my apprentice to pursue vampires is a risk I can no longer condone," he boomed. "As soon as he comes back, I'm taking him home."

"How did you know he went after the vampires?" Because the Grim Reaper had been watching us from the start, I realised. I should've known. "Did you see… Victoire?" I faltered, retreating from his looming shadow.

"It seems I have neglected to remind you that I am not answerable to your kind," he said.

"You aren't usually answerable to the vampires, either, but you let Victoire into your home." I could sense my family members' horrified stares, but my desire to spare Xavier his boss's wrath temporarily won out over self-preservation. "I *know* Victoire used to work with the Founders. She's the one who's responsible for Xavier leaving, too, because she's taken a new vampire hostage."

Luckily for all of us, Xavier chose that moment to appear, landing directly in front of his boss. "What are you doing here?"

"Looking for you," the Grim Reaper said. "You've neglected your duties for long enough."

"I was looking for a missing vampire," Xavier replied. "You know that the exposure of the magical world affects us too."

"No," the Grim Reaper said, his voice echoing around the lobby. "I will not take any more excuses from you. You're willing to put yourself on the line for your human companion, ahead of your duties."

"Please don't punish him for this." My hands curled into fists as the Grim Reaper's glare fixated on me. "He's telling the truth. He's trying to help the normals, not me."

"Did you expect me to forget that normal who you invited to live in the library?" he queried. "I know all about your little friend and her incurable condition and that you've been involving my apprentice in your futile attempts to save her." His words hit like thunderclaps.

"It's *not* futile, and it's none of your business."

A collective gasp arose among the others. I tensed, braced for the blow to fall, but the Grim Reaper didn't lay a shadowy finger on me. Instead, he spoke in a deceptively calm voice. "You must know that you'll never find what you're looking for at the vampires' home. They'd never have needed to create a cure. That poison is meant to kill."

Xavier started to speak, but the Grim Reaper cast a

shadow over his apprentice, and in a flood of darkness, they were gone.

No cure.

The words rang in my skull. Tears stung my eyes and tumbled down my face, and nobody else spoke for a long moment.

Then Maura cleared her throat. "So… is anyone going to address the manticore in the room? What's this cure? It's the same antidote that Victoire was talking about, I take it?"

"You heard?" I wiped my eyes on my sleeve. "The door was closed."

"I may have eavesdropped," Maura said. "I got curious. Look, I'm not trying to steal your secrets, but it didn't take much sleuthing to put two and two together. You were interested in that lab and the Founders' research, and Victoire implied that they have something you want."

I dropped my gaze, my face burning, feeling Cass's intense stare boring into me. "I know she was lying."

"Who, Victoire?" Cass asked sharply. "Did that vampire say the Founders had—"

"An antidote?" I finished. "She did, but she was probably trying to bait me."

"Exactly," Aunt Adelaide said. "Don't pay any attention to her, Cass—nor you, Rory."

"You think the Grim Reaper was right?" I asked in a choked voice.

"No," Cass growled. "That guy has no idea about the Founders. He's no vampire."

"No, but he knows them. He's as old as they are, if not older." I squeezed my eyes shut. "And I believe his word over Victoire's, to be honest."

"Oh, Rory." Estelle wrapped me in a hug. "They're both *awful* people. If you can even call them people. The Grim

Reaper is as bad as the vampires for emotional manipulation."

There is no cure. His words continued to reverberate inside my head, and I blinked back fresh tears. "That's it, then. We can't go after the Founders now, not unless Maura wants to go into their base alone."

"Not alone." Cass nodded to Maura. "Rory and I are coming with you."

"No, you certainly aren't," Aunt Adelaide said. "It's far too dangerous. The Founders have wanted to capture Rory from the start, and I expect the rest of us are next on the list."

"I know," I said.

The Founders wanted to read my mind and extract my secrets, from my dad's journal to the contents of the library itself. If I delivered myself to their doorstep, they would get all that and more.

Yet I could see that we would be playing into the Founders' hands no matter what decision we made. They'd figured out my emotional investment in Wynn's fate, and I wouldn't put it past them to kill her to spite me. No doubt, the Grim Reaper had known that, too, and that was why he'd removed Xavier from the playing field.

I *did* have one way to call him to my side, though—the stone he'd given me, which I could use to contact him in an emergency. If I was backed into a corner, even the Grim Reaper wouldn't be able to stop him from coming to help me.

"I say we go with Victoire, to let her pretend she's won us over," Cass said. "Then we'll use a lullaby charm when her back's turned. Maura can go into the house."

"Hey, I didn't agree to this," Maura said.

"She didn't," Estelle added, "and I thought you knew better, Cass."

"I can knock Victoire out before we even leave Ivory

Beach," Cass said. "We have the address, so we can go there without her."

"What about Evangeline?" I asked. "She wants revenge on Carlos Verdant. And she came to help us the last time we fought the Founders."

"She did," Cass agreed. "If she's on the fence, we'll work our powers of persuasion on her. I'm sure she won't object to us shutting Victoire into a coffin and taking matters into our own hands. She might even thank us for it."

"She might," I acknowledged. "But Maura really didn't agree to this."

"No, but I'm less at risk than the pair of you," Maura said. "And I'm intrigued enough to see what they're up to. Walking into obvious traps isn't my style, so if need be, I might decide to hop through the afterworld and ditch you. Fair warning."

"At least we know where we stand," Cass said. "How about you, Estelle?"

"What?" Estelle blanched. "No. I'm going to have to keep Aunt Candace occupied so she doesn't get the same idea."

Good point. If we'd had more time, I might have gone to see if the upstairs corridor might be able to help us, but its limits were unknown, and I didn't know if even its considerable powers would be able to help us when we were far from the library, surrounded by enemies.

As for finding a cure for Laney… that would have to wait until later. Even if no hope remained for her, I couldn't leave Wynn to suffer at the Founders' hands.

13

Half an hour later, Cass, Maura, and I walked back to the vampires' home. We'd hashed out our arguments to present to Evangeline, the effectiveness of which would depend on how thoroughly Victoire had annoyed her in the interim, and Cass had eagerly volunteered to cast a lullaby charm on the other vampire while her back was turned.

I didn't trust Victoire one bit, but the fact remained that she had far more information on the Founders than the rest of us did, and she also didn't have an angry Grim Reaper controlling her choices. For that reason, I had mixed feelings on the decision to knock her out, but it would probably serve us better in the long term.

Walking past the cemetery, I entertained the brief hope that Xavier would appear and join us after all, but not so much as a hint of shadow appeared. Nor was Victoire waiting outside Evangeline's house like she'd claimed she would be.

When I knocked on the door, Evangeline answered with her eyes narrowed. "What is it now?"

"Where's your friend?" I asked. "Does she know the Founders captured Wynn?"

"I haven't the faintest idea," she growled. "She left ten minutes ago."

"What?" My heart sank. "She left early?"

Had she gone to infiltrate the Founders or to rejoin them? Either way, we'd lost our chance to take her by surprise.

"Might I ask why that shocks you?" Evangeline enquired. "Victoire has always been out for herself and nobody else."

"What does she have to gain from getting involved in this, then?" I asked. "She's not going to rescue Wynn, I assume."

"I never did have access to her thoughts, Aurora," she said. "I cannot speak to her motives, but I sent a couple of my own people to confirm the veracity of her statement as to the Founders' location. They have not yet returned."

A shiver of unease passed over me. "Do you think they went inside the house? Or…?"

"Their loyalty is unmatched." A warning bite to her tone told me not to push her. "I shall wait a little longer before I send someone else."

"Why not go yourself?" I asked. "I thought you wanted to find Carlos Verdant."

"I will not play Victoire's games. If Carlos Verdant has indeed resurfaced, I will show myself to him in person and not as her pawn."

"Since when does following her make you her pawn?" This was all going wrong. "The Grim Reaper forced Xavier to stay behind, but Maura is still willing to come with us."

Without Evangeline, we were down yet another ally. I didn't fault my other family members for not getting involved, but with both the vampires' leader and Xavier gone, our odds of getting Wynn away from the Founders without a fight plummeted dramatically.

"I have certain rules I adhere to," she said. "Such as not

starting a feud in a location primarily inhabited by normals. My intention is for my allies to drive Verdant into *my* trap, not to walk into his own."

And what if your people have already fallen into his trap? From the way her eyes narrowed, she'd picked up on my thoughts, but I'd meant her to. "What about Wynn?"

"The new vampire is more trouble than she's worth," she said dispassionately. "I haven't the time to induct a normal into the magical world."

Anger sparked, and as she made to close the door, I stuck my foot in the way. "What was the point in you inviting Victoire into your home if you didn't intend to use any of her information?"

"You already know the answer to that, Aurora." She gave me a fanged smile reminiscent of Victoire herself. "She was useful."

This time, I let her close the door, my hands clenching and unclenching.

"Reading between the lines," Cass said, "she's planning to show up to our rescue at the last minute again."

"Is that her thing?" Maura asked from behind us. "Not sure I'd gamble on her bothering to show up, personally."

"You're the one who can jump through the shadows and escape if we're in a pinch," Cass pointed out. "Which we'll need if we want to find out what kind of trap her people ran into."

"You still want to go ahead with this?" I looked between Maura and Cass. "Both of you?"

"We've come this far." Cass turned away from the vampires' house. "I'll use a transportation spell. I'm not going through the afterworld."

"Your funeral if they've booby-trapped the place," Maura commented. "I'm likely to be immune to any magical defences they might have used, but you two aren't."

She had a point, but I didn't want to go through the afterworld with anyone other than Xavier, and I didn't particularly want to let Cass run into a trap alone either. "I'll risk it. Meet you there."

"See you on the other side." Maura vanished, while I pulled out my wand.

Here we go. I pictured the street adjacent to Bailey's house, and in a wave of our wands, Ivory Beach once again disappeared.

Cass and I landed on a street corner. I didn't see Maura, but Cass began striding away as though she knew the place.

"Cass," I hissed. "Wait. Welling Street is… that way."

I had to check the maps app on my phone to make sure we were going in the right direction, but it took little time for us to catch up to Maura. She was hovering on a street corner, a perturbed frown on her face.

"I don't see Evangeline's vampires," she said. "Or anyone else, either. I scoped out the house, but the curtains are drawn, so I don't know which room they're keeping Wynn in."

Figures. "We'll get closer. Don't they have any security guards or at least a ward?"

"Not that I could see, but they'll want to avoid drawing the normals' attention, I'm betting," she murmured. "They'll have all their booby traps on the other side of the front gate."

I cast an unseen spell on myself, and Cass did likewise. The streets were quiet as we made our way toward the large, grand house that Maura had pointed out. A tall gate stood between us and the path leading to the front door, thick hedges circling the front garden and preventing us from seeing much of the house. That was probably the point.

"I'll try to peek through the windows, but I'll need to go inside to see what's going on," Maura muttered. "You two wait in that alley over there while I find out where the humans are being held prisoner. Then we'll plan for how to get them out."

"All right," I said.

Tension thrummed inside me, and even Cass gave no argument. We ducked into the narrow alleyway alongside the property while Maura vanished into shadow. Even with the unseen spell averting my attention from her face, Cass radiated disapproval at being asked to hide behind a hedge while Maura did all the sneaking around.

A long minute trailed by before Maura reappeared, grim-faced. "I found Wynn, but there's a slight issue. She isn't the only prisoner."

"More normals?" I guessed. "Or new vampires?"

"The latter." She took in a breath. "That Victoire is in there too. Locked in the same cell as the newbie vampires."

"She's a prisoner?" *No way.* "Are you sure she isn't pretending?"

If not, how had Carlos Verdant and his allies managed to capture *her?* And what about Evangeline's allies?

"I don't care if she is," Cass hissed. "We need to know which room they're in."

"Upper left, but it's going to be impossible to get that Wynn out of her prison without Victoire noticing. They're all in the same room."

Oh boy. "Where's Carlos Verdant?"

"Not upstairs," she replied. "I heard at least four voices from downstairs, but I can't sense vampires the way I can humans, and I'd have got caught if I'd materialised in every room. That's the best I could do."

"It helps." I drew in a breath. "All right. The quickest way is probably for you to get Wynn out through the afterworld. I know she won't find it a pleasant experience, but it's better than drawing the attention of all the vampires in the house at once."

"And the other prisoners?" Maura queried. "I can grab two people at a time, max, and after I rescue the first pair, I'll be lucky to have five seconds before Victoire or someone else raises the alarm."

Ah. "Maybe we should have waited for Evangeline."

I hadn't known Victoire would go to those lengths to lay a trap for us, but Wynn was still alive, and right now, we were the only people who could get her out of there. Trap or no trap, her life might be forfeit at the slightest whim on behalf of her captors.

Cass grabbed my arm. "Someone's outside."

I lifted my gaze, peering through the thick hedge as movement stirred outside the front door. Either the vampires had heard Maura's entrance, or they'd been keeping an eye out for more intruders after they'd caught Evangeline's allies. And Victoire, assuming she was a prisoner at all.

A colossal shadow fell over the alleyway, blotting out the sunlight. Beside me, Maura sucked in a breath. "No way."

The shadow spread wider, bringing a chill that couldn't be mistaken. *It can't be possible.*

A shadowy figure stepped out of the darkness and closed the distance between us in a heartbeat. Icy fingers closed around my upper arm, dragging me away from the others, and shadows wrapped around my body from behind, rendering me immobile.

"Hey!"

Light flashed—Cass's wand—but was swiftly extinguished with a muffled yelp as someone knocked her off her feet. I glimpsed blurred figures moving around her and Maura. *Vampires.*

Twisting my arm, I tried to free myself from my captor's hold. I'd come prepared to fight vampires but not a Reaper. This one was strong, and the numbing chill of the afterworld

locked my body to the spot. I couldn't even see my oppo-
nent's face, but I was familiar enough with the sensation to
know when the afterworld pulled both of us into its
embrace.

152

14

Through the darkness, an amused voice spoke. "What have we here? A trespasser, willingly delivering herself into our hands?"

A familiar face greeted me when the darkness of the afterworld faded, revealing a wide hallway. Ahead, Carlos Verdant stood in front of a room cast in shadow, regarding me with a mixture of curiosity and annoyance. "Aurora Hawthorn. You weren't content to destroy my countryside home? You had to come for my safe house too?"

"You're capturing normals—" I broke off in a yelp when two pairs of hands grabbed me again, roughly pulling off my cloak and relieving me of my wand, my Biblio-Witch Inventory, my notebook and pen, and even the stone Xavier had given me. *Oh no.*

"That's better," Carlos Verdant said. "You can wait upstairs while we deal with the other trespassers."

The two figures behind me—vampires—shoved me down the hallway. One seized my arm in a grip that warned that if I tried to get away, I'd end up with a broken wrist or worse, and steered me toward a wide stairway.

I hope Maura and Cass escaped, I thought as the two vampires herded me upstairs. A short distance down the landing, we came to a door, which my captors unlocked. The vampire holding my arm shoved me over the threshold, causing me to stumble into the room.

As the lock clicked behind me, two sights struck me at once: Wynn and another few terrified humans, huddled in a corner—and Victoire, lounging against the wall, with her mouth curved in its customary grin.

"You too?" she asked.

"Did they… actually capture you?" I stood rigidly in the doorway, conscious of being trapped in the same room as a predator—several, if the other vampires were part of the ambush too. "I thought you were Carlos's apprentice."

Victoire laughed. "Oh, silly human. I burned that bridge a long time ago… though not in quite as literal a sense as what you did to his house."

It can't be. "What are they going to do to us?"

They wouldn't turn *me* into a vampire, surely, but that didn't mean they intended to leave me unharmed. Far from it.

She laughed. "When they've extracted any useful information that you can give them, I expect they'll dispose of you. Like me, you're too much trouble to keep alive."

"You don't seem that bothered." I could only assume Cass and Maura were on their way to fetch help, but there were no guarantees that my family members would make it here in time to rescue me, let alone without getting caught themselves.

Worse, I couldn't call Xavier to my side, because the vampires had taken off my cloak, along with the stone he'd given me. *What was I thinking?*

"I'm surprised your other family members didn't come with you," Victoire said, evidently picking up on my thoughts. "They didn't want to risk themselves for the sake of a few mere normals, I suppose."

I lifted my gaze to the corner where Wynn and three others huddled—vampires, but new and terrified.

"Nobody knew the Founders had a *Reaper* working with them." I dragged my attention back to Victoire's smirking face. "Did you know?"

Before she could answer, the door clicked open again, and Carlos Verdant reappeared. At the sight of the naked fury on his face, my heart gave a spasm of fear.

"Come with me, Aurora," he commanded.

I wondered if the others would try to run while the door was open, but nobody so much as moved an inch when he grabbed my arm and dragged me out of the room. His typical vampire's iron grip ensured I didn't have any chance to free myself until we reached the adjacent room, where he shoved me into a wooden chair and closed the door behind us. A lock clicked into place, just in case I'd had any idle thoughts of escape.

The room itself contained nothing but a couple of wooden chairs, one of which Carlos Verdant sat down in. No other furniture occupied the wide space—nothing to use as a weapon or to put between me and the vampire. The curtains were drawn, cutting off all natural light and creating shadows thick enough to contain a Reaper—but the Founders' new ally didn't need to be present for me to be in serious trouble.

Carlos Verdant surveyed me for a moment. "I confess I didn't know the true value of your family's knowledge when we first met, Aurora."

"You mean when you kidnapped my aunt and cousin?" My voice trembled despite my best efforts. "What do you want with me?"

His pitch-dark eyes bored into mine. "I heard from a

friend of mine that you have in your possession a journal that is of great interest to my fellow vampires."

Dammit. Had he spoken to Mortimer Vale? Surely not— Vale and his allies were in jail—but the incident at Ridgeway House had hardly been inconspicuous, and it wouldn't have taken much poking around to reveal that my family had been involved both in Vale's imprisonment and in the destruction of the Founders' base. And that was assuming Victoire hadn't been an informant herself.

"I don't have the journal with me." I spoke clearly, my gaze on the ceiling instead of on his face. "You took everything I had."

That was the problem. I couldn't use my family's magic without access to my Biblio-Witch Inventory or at least a pen, I couldn't call Xavier without the stone, and even if I'd persuaded Cass to give me her anti–mind-reading pendant, he could simply have removed it from me as well.

"Your family has quite the unique strain of magic," he said. "Biblio-witches… I believe your family must be unique in the magical world."

I said nothing. The less I spoke, the less I gave away.

"Fascinating." He leaned closer to me. I focused on my breathing, on not letting any wayward thoughts slip into my mind. "You've been practising at resisting vampires, haven't you?"

"There's nothing useful in the journal," I told him. "It's mostly my dad's accounts of his travels. There's nothing you don't already know."

"I very much doubt that, Aurora," he said. "Even if it's true, the journal lists several *very* valuable books… including one that your family stole from my fellow vampires."

Still, I said nothing. Carlos Verdant wasn't one of Mortimer Vale's friends, and he hadn't known of the book *or* the journal when we first met. The Founders kept as many secrets from each other as they did from the rest of us, and I suspected that Verdant wouldn't have taken an interest in me at all if not for the fact that I'd burned down his house.

His smile broadened. "Let's see…"

I blinked repeatedly, my attention fixed on the ceiling, but he loomed closer until it was impossible *not* to look at his face. Teeth bared, he reached down with a hand and pushed my chin upward until our eyes locked. Watery terror swept over me, and my breath stopped. *He's going to bite me.*

"No, I am not," he said. "I have no intention of turning *you,* as amusing as it might be to become your sire."

Sire. That must be how he'd recaptured Wynn. Maybe the same went for Victoire too.

"I have to thank you for delivering both of my wayward progeny to me, Aurora," he said. "Though I do wish you hadn't destroyed my lab. Some of those potions took decades to create."

"Why potions?" I spoke through gritted teeth as his icy fingers dug into my chin, making it hard to keep my thoughts locked away. "What was the point in turning normals into vampires only to torture them?"

"Knowledge, of course," he said. "I heard you fell into possession of one of our manuscripts recently too. Poor Cateline…"

Unbidden, his words conjured up a rush of images that I struggled to stifle. No doubt that was the point, but how to keep him from glimpsing my secrets when every thought in my mind had the potential to turn into a weapon that could be used against my family? Even if I somehow managed to keep him from guessing the reasons for my personal interest in the Founders' experiments, my family's other secrets waited in the wings. My dad's journal was the least of them. There was the fourth-floor corridor, the nature of the library itself—

No. If he grasped the true nature of the library, there was nothing to stop him from sending his fellow vampires to pillage the place. I had to keep him from delving that deep into my thoughts, even if it meant revealing something I didn't want anyone to see in the process.

I envisioned the secrets clustered in my mind as a ball of thread threatening to unspool, and I intentionally picked one thread and tugged. Just a little. Enough to pique his interest.

"Oh?" Carlos Verdant's expression sharpened with hunger. "Your friend was turned into a vampire against her will?"

"Thanks to your people." I let the thread continue to unspool, slowly, and his hungry expression intensified.

"Oh, what a tragedy." He spoke in tones more suitable for someone who'd stumbled upon a buried fortune. "Turned into a vampire, poisoned… and left for dead."

"She's not dead." As a sudden surge of anger on Laney's behalf caused me to temporarily forget the terror of being that close to a vampire, I seized on the chance to further bury the library's secrets beneath my own. "It's your people's fault she's in that state."

He released me, surprise flitting across his face. "So *fierce,* Aurora."

"Did you create the poison?" I choked out the words. Instinct told me to guard my emotions, but if it meant sparing the rest of my family, I would gladly suffer the humiliation. He couldn't do anything else to Laney. Not anymore.

"Yes, I did," he replied. "There's no antidote, you know… I'm rather proud of that one."

No antidote. Even after hearing the same from the Grim Reaper, his words struck me like a blow. Breathing hard, I sat upright in my chair, a surge of guilt and pain constricting my chest.

Carlos Verdant's brow scrunched up as he looked into my eyes again, and he shook his head in disgust. "Humans. Too attached to their emotions."

Yes. We are. And right now, they were all I had. I thought of Laney, thought of my family, and forced out all other images.

"You've given me enough to work with for now," he said. "I'll check in with my Reaper friend and see if she's managed to track down your wayward family members. For now, you'll return to your cell."

"The Reaper." I gasped when he seized my upper arm and yanked me out of my seat. "How did you recruit a Reaper?"

"How indeed," he said. "I think I'll let her explain that for herself. It'll give you something to look forward to, before the end."

In a blur, he dragged me out of the room and across the corridor. When the door to the prison closed behind me, I looked up into Victoire's violet eyes and jumped back in alarm.

"Can you not do that?" I rasped. "It's creepy."

She grinned, exposing her pointed teeth. "Honestly, Aurora, we're on the same side. Unless you'd prefer not to be."

Fear washed over me. In the wake of my interrogation at Carlos Verdant's hands, I'd momentarily forgotten the danger presented by my fellow prisoner, but there was nothing to stop her from biting me here and now and leaving me to die without anyone coming to my rescue.

"Relax, Aurora." She laughed. "I have no intention of killing you."

"Carlos Verdant does."

His ally was a full-blown Reaper—not half, like Maura, or an apprentice, like Xavier. Why she would ally with the vampires was a question that I dearly wanted the answer to, but I had the suspicion that answers would only be presented to me when the Reaper came for my soul.

"I expect he'll want to extract your secrets first," she said. "You successfully kept him from penetrating your deepest thoughts?"

Yes... for now. He hadn't found out the library's secrets, but I'd had to expose Laney's conundrum in order to steer his attention away from my family, which left a bad taste in my mouth. Laney herself would have encouraged me to do exactly that—she didn't care about her own personal secrets being broadcast for the whole world to hear—but guilt assailed me all the same, and I knew Victoire would be able to sense some of my inner turmoil.

"He said the Reaper's gone after my family," I said to distract her attention. "That means she might not be in the house at the moment."

"The Reaper isn't here?" A calculating smile curled her lip. "I thank you for that information, Aurora."

"Erm... you're welcome." I glanced at the door. "Can't your vampire super strength break us out?"

"I *could*," she said, "but it'd be messy, and there are less conspicuous means of escape. I thought your family had a way with words."

Words. Of course... But there were no writing tools or materials in the cell as they'd taken my notebook and pen as well as my Biblio-Witch Inventory.

"You can write with anything, right?" She bared her teeth invitingly. "Including blood?"

"Please don't bite me."

"I can give you some of mine instead."

"No thanks." Vampire blood was potent enough that they didn't just hand it out except to people they wanted to turn. Despite my current vulnerability, I had zero desire to join the ranks of the undead myself.

"What's life without a little risk?" Victoire smiled. "Ah… our esteemed host is back."

The door opened a moment later, and this time, Carlos Verdant beckoned to Victoire. "It's about time we got to the point, isn't it?"

I half expected her to put up a fight, but she didn't. Victoire departed, leaving me alone with the terrified normals. I waited for a moment, scanning the room for anything that might serve as a writing instrument and finding none.

"Hey," I whispered to Wynn. "Do you have anything on you? Anything I can write with?"

She simply watched me, blank-eyed and unseeing. The others regarded me in the same manner, without a hint of emotion in their expressions, not even fear or anger at their predicament. They were all in Carlos Verdant's thrall, and I hadn't a clue how to break a vampire sire's hold on those he'd turned, if it was even possible.

Victoire isn't under his spell. Not that she could help me at the moment, either. I had to act, preferably before the Reaper returned, but how? My family must have been trying to get to me, but they were stymied by the Reaper chasing them and would have a hard job keeping from being captured themselves—Maura too.

No, I would have to get out of here myself. I might not get through another interrogation without Carlos Verdant penetrating deeper into my thoughts. In my mental inventory of information that I least wanted the Founders to find out, my family's secrets and the library's true nature would be at the very top of that list. How many more interrogation sessions would it take for him to break me?

The sound of a commotion came from down the corridor. I held my breath, straining my ears as I made out the unmistakable noise of shouting and thumping. *Is that…?*

"We're okay," I whispered to the other vampires. "Please try to resist Carlos Verdant's control. I'm pretty sure we're about to be rescued."

I listened, trying to make out my family members' voices, but I couldn't hear them or Maura. *Please tell me the Reaper didn't follow them here.*

The door clicked open, and Victoire came sauntering in. "Well, Aurora, I believe thanks are in order."

Wait... it's her? "What did you do?"

"I locked our host inside his study," she said. "And his allies are currently locked in the downstairs room. Now you can call your family to rescue your baby vampires."

"With what?" When she threw something at me, I reached out a hand, catching the pen between my fingertips.

More loud crashes came from downstairs.

"I believe our hosts have escaped," she said. "Or their shadowy friend has returned. Move swiftly, Aurora."

Hastily, I pressed the point of the pen to the nearest surface—the wall—and scratched out the word *summon.*

In a flash of light, my cloak appeared in a heap on the floor. As I scrambled to pick it up, shadows stirred behind Victoire, painting a long stretch of darkness on the floor— the Reaper.

"Xavier!" I slung the coat over my shoulder and slid my hand into the pocket, my fingers brushing against the stone he'd given me. *Xavier!*

The Reaper's shadow loomed over me—and a scythe slammed down between us as Xavier emerged from the darkness in full-on angel of death mode. My heart lifted as the other Reaper retreated from his scythe. I still couldn't see her face, but she didn't appear to have a weapon of her own. *Because she's a rogue, maybe.*

Victoire beckoned to me. "Come on, Aurora."

"I can't leave the others." The other prisoners hadn't

budged, not even with the fight between two Reapers erupting outside their door. They might as well have been statues.

"Don't you want to save yourself?" She pursed her lips. "All right."

She vanished at speed, darting around the Reapers, while I turned back toward the prisoners. How could I get them out of there? Xavier and the Reaper were fighting in a blur of shadow, entirely blocking the path to the stairs, but I would have a job and a half hauling four reluctant vampires outside single-handedly.

Another shadow appeared at my back, in the doorway. "Sorry for the holdup," Maura said. "That Reaper is persistent."

"Help me get them out." I gestured to the other vampires huddled in the corner. "They're under the vampire's control. He's their sire."

Maura swore. "I'll help them."

"I don't think so." Carlos Verdant appeared, having run straight past the battling Reapers, his teeth bared in fury.

15

The vampires stirred at the appearance of their sire, all their eyes turning in his direction, their expressions blank. *Oh no.* Xavier and the Reaper had vanished, and Maura and I stood side by side against the vampire and his allies.

But one of those allies was Wynn, turned against her will, and her companions were no doubt equally powerless to resist their sire.

"Run!" I shouted, grabbing my wand. I didn't have time to think before I cast a spell—a freeze-frame—that stopped Carlos Verdant in his tracks. The other vampires went still, freed from their master's command, but nobody ran. *Ah crap.* How was Maura supposed to get all of them out of here at the same time?

A loud crash sounded from somewhere downstairs, the sound of a door being opened with force. Hoping it was my family arriving and not the other vampires breaking out of the room that Victoire had locked them in, I pointed my wand at Carlos Verdant and cast a knockback spell that pushed him out of the way of the door. Then I cast a second freeze-frame spell on him in case the first one wore off.

"Come on!" I beckoned to the other vampires, but nobody so much as stirred. "Maura?"

"On it." She darted into the room and grabbed two of the dazed newbie vampires by the arms.

The three of them vanished into the afterworld, but I'd hardly had time to blink before soft footsteps sounded on the stairs. *Crap. It's the other vampires.*

The three vampires reached the landing and spread out to block my path of escape. Carlos Verdant would break free of my spell at any second, and I couldn't think clearly enough to devise a way of taking out all of them at once.

Then again, not being able to think would lessen the chances of the vampires reading my thoughts and anticipating my next move.

The vampires rushed me, and I waved my wand to cast a smokescreen spell. Smoke billowed out, obscuring the upper landing. Pointing my wand into the smoke, I cast a lullaby charm. I couldn't see who I was aiming at, but the thud of a body against the soft carpet told me I'd hit at least one of my targets.

As Maura reappeared in a shadowy blur, one of the vampires shouted, "Fire!"

My heart lurched, but I realised a moment later that there weren't any flames—my smokescreen spell had made them think I'd initiated a repeat of what I'd done to Carlos's other house. I didn't dare use any *actual* firedust with a bunch of innocent newbie vampires stuck in here, but the general confusion gave Maura the chance to seize the remaining new vampires and vanish into the afterworld.

Time to go. I ran after her but collided with a solid form. Carlos Verdant's furious face loomed at me out of the smoke, his hand reaching to grasp my shoulder. "You have some nerve, starting a fire in my house again."

"It's not a fire." I squirmed, pain rippling up my arm. "Let me go."

"I don't think so." He hauled me across the landing and shoved me into the room in which he'd questioned me. "I wonder if you and your allies would be as quick to vandalise my property if you knew that I could command that poor normal to die at any moment?"

"What?" I squirmed, unable to free myself. "Because you're her sire, right?"

"That's right." His teeth bared in a cross between a snarl and a smile. "She and the others all carry capsules of poison. You should know what kind."

I stopped struggling, my heart sinking. *That poison...* There was no cure.

"That's right," he crooned. "If you'd rather they join your friend in eternal sleep, please continue to resist me, Aurora."

"No."

Anguish rose inside me. I couldn't risk Wynn or the others, but if I died here, Laney would never awaken. I would never get to see if the library could pull off the impossible.

"It's up to you." His teeth hovered over my throat. "I'll make it painless, Aurora, as a courtesy."

A rush of darkness engulfed the room, and Carlos Verdant abruptly released my shoulder. Shadows masked the vampire from sight, and a solid hand gripped mine, holding me tight, pulling me through the darkness. *Xavier.*

The shadows faded, but Xavier's grip on my hand remained. We'd landed on the pavement outside the vampires' house, and Carlos Verdant was nowhere in sight.

"Wait!" I gasped. "He was going to order those other vampires to take poison and die."

"He'll have a hard time doing that from the afterworld." Xavier's face was ghostly pale in the dimming light. "Are you all right?"

"I'm fine, but the others—" I broke off. "Wait, where's the other Reaper?"

"She ran off," he said. "She didn't have a scythe, and I think she must have realised her allies were losing."

"Speaking of allies…" I gestured toward the house. "There are three more vampires in there."

"Good." Cass came running up to join us. "I was looking for a fight."

She sprinted through the now-open gate to the house just as Aunt Adelaide and Estelle ran around the corner too.

"Cass, stop!" Aunt Adelaide called breathlessly. "How many vampires, Rory?"

"Three," I replied. "Carlos Verdant is stuck in the afterworld. Right, Xavier?"

"Yes." His expression darkened. "Unfortunately, since vampires don't need to breathe, he's capable of surviving the experience. If his Reaper ally comes back…"

"Go and make sure he doesn't." I squeezed his hand. "I'll be okay."

As Xavier vanished, Estelle ran over and hugged me. "Sorry we took so long, Rory."

"Rory?" Maura called to me across the street. Huddled behind her were the four vampires she'd rescued. "What should I do with them?"

"Take them to the authorities," Aunt Adelaide answered promptly. "Estelle and I will help once we've handled the vampires left in the house."

The pair of them hurried through the front gate, while I ran across the street to join Maura. Wynn and the other vampires were no longer under their sire's control, but they remained huddled in a terrified group behind Maura. They needed help and guidance, and unfortunately, the only person capable of providing that help that I knew of was Evangeline.

"Having trouble?" Victoire was back, her approach as sudden and startling as a Reaper's. All the vampires jumped.

"You again?" Maura eyed Victoire. "I thought you were a prisoner too."

"I was," she said. "It seems to me that you need help rounding up those vampires. Am I right in thinking that you want to escort them to Evangeline?"

I hesitated. The answer was yes, but I still didn't entirely trust her, even if she *had* helped me escape. "What, you're going to walk them all the way back to Ivory Beach?"

"If you'd prefer to use a transportation spell, I can help make sure nobody runs off," she offered. "It'd be a shame for any of them to end up stranded in the normal world after their ordeal, wouldn't it?"

She didn't sound entirely sincere, but Maura couldn't carry all of them through the afterworld simultaneously, and I wasn't confident enough in my abilities with transportation spells to bring four people with me at the same time.

"I'll take two of them to Evangeline," Maura offered. "You can take the other two—oh, dammit."

The vampires *moved*. All four of them sprinted in different directions as though they'd been given instructions nobody else could hear.

"What the—" I made to cross the road, but I had zero idea which one of them to chase. They'd run too quickly for my eye to track all their movements at once. "Did Carlos Verdant escape?"

"I'll find them." Maura vanished into the afterworld.

Victoire lifted her head as though listening for something too far away for me to hear. "I wonder…"

"You can hear them?" I guessed. "Where are they?"

I hadn't a hope of catching up to the vampires on foot, but Victoire was a different story. She pointed across the road then ran in that direction, fast enough that I could barely see her. I jogged after her, assailed by doubts. *Should I be running after a vampire alone?*

"Aurora," Victoire called from around a street corner. "It's… her. Wynn."

I followed the sound of her voice and came to an abrupt halt. Wynn lay flat on her back, her eyes wide open and unseeing. A gleam of red at the corner of her mouth told me her fate.

"No… *No.*" I dropped to my knees beside her. "How? Carlos Verdant is supposed to be—trapped."

"He must have escaped." Victoire leaned over me, placing her hand on my shoulder. "I'm sorry, Aurora."

I tensed, not liking to be touched by *any* vampire. "Where are the others?"

As I straightened upright, Victoire's grip on my shoulder tightened. In a sudden swooping motion, she lifted me into her arms at such an angle that I couldn't reach my wand or anything else in my pocket.

"Hey!" I squirmed. "Let me go!"

"Now, don't struggle, Aurora, dear," she said. "You should know better than to resist."

"What are you doing?" *Capturing me* was the obvious answer, but why? "You aren't working with them. They locked you up too."

"Not all Founders are on the same side, are they?"

Oh no. As the realisation sank in, she laughed and broke into a run. The world blurred around me as I struggled to think through the sweeping dizziness. If she wasn't on Carlos Verdant's side, there was only one explanation. She was with Mortimer Vale.

After a long stretch of dizzying speed, we came to a stop on a deserted country lane, bordered by fields and trees and not much else. No signs of human habitation were in sight.

"Where... *are* we?"

"This isn't our new base," Victoire said. "I merely brought you somewhere remote enough that nobody will come looking for you."

Xavier will. My family will. They would find a way, or I would escape. I just had to stall her until I figured out a way out. "Why'd you really come to Ivory Beach?"

"Surely you've worked it out, Aurora... though it was fun to wind up Evangeline too." A soft laugh escaped her. "She knew I was playing games with her but not the extent to which I would be willing to go in order to gain what I desire."

"You didn't try to get into the library."

"Oh, there was no point in trying that until after you'd told me how to crack the defences," she said. "I've had ample opportunity to look around from the outside, though it became considerably easier to avoid attention when your friend slipped into a coma. Do you recall receiving a letter some time ago?"

The letter... from Mortimer Vale. She was the one who'd delivered his threatening message. Had she been visiting him in jail the whole time?

"Dear Mortimer is quite ticked off with you, Aurora." She planted my feet on the ground, her hands grasping my upper arms and preventing me from moving so much as an inch.

"He deserved what he got," I gasped, my prey instincts kicking in. *I can't let her into my thoughts.*

"You'd make a good vampire, Aurora." She peered down at me. "I know you were holding back from sharing with Carlos... an admirable effort, but not enough for me."

"Even if you extract all my secrets, the library's defences

won't let you through," I told her. "Mortimer Vale failed, and so will you."

"We'll see," she said. "I can break you in a thousand ways, Aurora, until you give me what I desire."

"Maybe I'd rather die."

She leaned closer. "Ah, but who would save your friend then?"

I squeezed my eyes shut. "She can't be saved. Carlos Verdant was right."

I could sense her trying to probe my thoughts, but since I'd let my emotions keep Carlos Verdant from accessing my deeper thoughts, maybe the same trick would work on her—anything other than giving up the secrets of the library that belonged to my family alone.

"Your library is a mine of information," she crooned. "Let me in."

No. An image came into my mind's eye of the guardian of the fourth-floor corridor standing in front of the door. If only I'd had an equivalent to keep the vampires out of my thoughts, I might have been able to stop her from getting in, but any second now, she would slip past and into the depths of my mind.

"Don't be like that, Aurora." She tutted. "What is that? Some creation of your family's?"

"What's what?" I opened my eyes to see her peering at my face, a furrow in her brow. "Did you see…?"

Had she seen the guardian? If so, the guardian itself might intrigue her enough to distract from the other secrets hiding behind the corridor. Figuring it was worth a shot, I pictured the shapeless figure standing in the way of the door, preventing her from getting inside.

To my surprise, her grip loosened enough for me to free one hand. Plunging my fist into my pocket, I seized the first object that my fingers brushed against—my wand—and jabbed it upward at her face.

I hadn't had time to cast a spell, but sparks flew outward and caused her to recoil. Tugging my other arm free, I cast a lullaby charm, and Victoire dropped like a stone.

Applause rang out in the empty street. Evangeline walked into view, offering me a smile. "I'll take it from here, Aurora."

"How long have you been standing there?"

"Only long enough to see you resist her." She smiled again. "It was masterful."

"You knew she was going to betray us." I couldn't keep the accusation out of my voice. "She wasn't with Carlos Verdant."

"Oh, he's in trouble too." Evangeline swooped over and gathered Victoire in her arms as though she was a child.

"Rory!" Xavier came running up to me. "Was she—"

"With Mortimer Vale," I said. "She was going to try to get into the library."

But I'd stopped her. Whether through a fluke or not, I'd kept her from penetrating my deepest thoughts. As I watched, Evangeline lifted Victoire bodily and sprinted away, leaving Xavier and me alone on the street.

"Where's Carlos Verdant?" My throat tightened. "He ordered the other vampires to die, didn't he? It was him."

I didn't know why he hadn't given the same order to Victoire. Maybe he'd retained some fondness toward her due to their shared history.

Xavier inclined his head. "He slipped through my fingers, but I caught him again, and I handed him to my boss."

"You gave him to the Grim Reaper?" The image of a vampire being imprisoned in the Reaper's house… Well, it was strangely fitting. "And… my family?"

"Back at the house, rounding up the vampires." Xavier reached for my arm. "I'll take you back."

"How did you know where to find me?" That was the obvious question. "You followed Evangeline?"

"No, I can't sense her, remember?" he said. "I sensed you. You didn't touch the stone, but I knew how to find you."

Warmth spread through me despite the lingering chill. "I'm glad you did."

"Me too." He drew me closer. "We should go home."

16

It wasn't until we reached the library that I thought to ask Xavier another obvious question. "Where's the Reaper?"

"Gone." His expression darkened. "She slipped away into the afterworld when I was handing Verdant to my boss, and I got distracted when I realised you'd gone."

"You can go and look for her now. I'll be fine." I indicated the library doorway, where Aunt Adelaide was beckoning me inside. "My family's there."

"All right." He hugged me tightly, and I squeezed him back. Then he vanished into the afterworld, while I entered the library to join my family. Typically, Aunt Candace, who'd stayed behind, was bombarding the others with questions.

"This isn't any good at all!" she was saying. "I can't write a novel based on such paltry details."

"You're the one who had other priorities," Estelle said. "We were more interested in getting Rory away from the vampires than taking notes."

"Did you get anything else out of the fourth-floor corridor while we were gone?" Cass asked her.

"No." Aunt Candace scowled. "Like we thought, it only answers one request per day."

"One from each of us, I assume," Cass said. "I wonder…"

"Not now," Aunt Adelaide said wearily. "We'll look closer at that corridor tomorrow, after everyone's had time to recover from today's ordeal. Rory, where's that other Reaper? Maura?"

"I assume she went back to the hotel," Estelle said. "Unless she's with Xavier…"

"Chasing the other Reaper?" I guessed. "I don't know who *she* was, but we're going to be in real trouble if the Founders have started working with the Reapers."

"She didn't have a scythe," Cass remarked. "That makes her a rogue, and one who'll be in trouble herself if the Reaper authorities catch up to her. I'd say we let the Grim Reaper make an example of her."

"If he can find her," I replied. "Hmm. I wonder if she's the one the Grim Reaper originally sensed when he thought there was a rogue in the area."

"Maybe." Aunt Adelaide's expression shadowed. "Either way, he's better equipped to catch that rogue than the rest of us are."

True. "He's also got Carlos Verdant sitting in his house. Xavier shoved him into the afterworld."

"Good," Estelle said. "I hope he's scared half to death."

"Yeah." A spasm of guilt hit me. "When he got out, he ordered Wynn and the others to take poison and die."

"Oh." Estelle's face fell. "I did wonder what happened to them… I was too busy chasing Verdant's allies out of the house to keep track."

"I suspected," Aunt Adelaide said. "I'm sorry, Rory."

"It's nobody's fault except his." I lowered my gaze, my eyes stinging. "I know… they'd have had a hard time adapting to the magical world anyway. Not everyone is like…"

Like Laney. Whose secrets I'd betrayed to Verdant to avoid exposing the library.

Estelle wrapped me in a hug. "It's not your fault either. I know what you're thinking."

"That's not it." I squeezed my eyes shut. "Verdant interrogated me, and... I was so desperate to keep him from accessing the library that I had to let him partway in. He knows about Laney."

"Who doesn't?" The challenging question came from Cass. When I opened my eyes, she was scowling at me. "It's hardly news to anyone familiar with our family. Better than him knowing how to reach the hidden corridor."

"Speaking of which..." Aunt Adelaide turned away. "I believe my sister has gone upstairs again."

"Not again." I figured Aunt Candace must have slipped away while we'd been talking. "At least she can't make another wish until the morning."

I didn't betray the library... but had that entirely been my own doing? Had it been coincidental that I'd thought of the guardian and Victoire had been unable to get past that image? I didn't know, but I was too tired to think on the repercussions of that.

"You're safe," Estelle said. "That's the important part, Rory. Nobody can fault you for doing what you needed to do to stay alive."

No. I'd wanted to survive not just for my own sake but for Laney's. For the sliver of hope that remained that I might be able to save her.

———

The following morning brought a predictable interruption in the form of Maura materialising in the lobby. This time, her brother appeared at her side, and he immediately flew into the stacks and disappeared.

"Mart, enough," she said. "Don't run off."

"What's the problem?" His ghostly head popped up from between the shelves. "I never had the chance to explore."

"We'll have to come back some other time," she told him. "We need to go home today, and… I mean, I'm assuming we'll be welcome back here again," she added to me. "I'll understand if not."

"Of course you'll be welcome back here," I said. "The same can't be said for the *other* Reaper. Do you know if Xavier caught her?"

"Nope," she replied. "I helped for a bit, but I was exhausted, frankly. Your boyfriend was way more dedicated. He's not half human like me, though."

"True." Xavier must have been out chasing that Reaper all night. While he didn't need sleep, technically, I felt bad for him. "I hope he caught her. A rogue Reaper working with the vampires…"

"It's a new one for me too," Maura said. "Though if more Reapers have been involved with the Founders in the past, it might explain how certain people might have been able to figure out how to stop my Reaper abilities from working. It takes one Reaper to beat another, after all."

"It can't be a widespread issue." I *hoped* it wasn't. "If it is…"

"The Reaper Council will take action. I'll make them do it myself." Maura lifted her hand and waved across the lobby. "There's your cousin and your aunt. Take care of them, Rory. They're good people."

"Yeah," I said. "They are."

"Maura." Aunt Adelaide reached us first. "Are you leaving?"

"Yes," Maura replied. "I just wanted to thank all of you for the help."

"We didn't really help you find what you needed, though," I said apologetically. "Instead, you got dragged into our drama."

"Or she walked into it willingly," Mart interjected. "She always does that."

Maura gave him a rude gesture. "I do have a list of questions to ask the Reaper Council, at least. Concerning our rogue. I'm sure they'll be thrilled with me."

"As thrilled as the Grim Reaper?" Estelle guessed. "Glad you were around to help us last night."

"Anytime." Maura waved one last time then walked out of the library, her ghostly brother trailing behind her.

"Glad she's gone," Cass remarked after a moment's pause. "Reapers are bad news."

I raised a brow. "*All* Reapers?"

"You know what I mean," she said. "Ah, speaking of whom… There's your Reaper beau."

I spun back to the door, where Xavier had appeared.

"Sorry, Rory," he said. "My boss is—"

Darkness wreathed the area as the Grim Reaper appeared behind his apprentice, his towering form blotting out all the light.

"Right behind me," Xavier finished.

Ah. My mouth parted. "Can I help you?"

"You can start," he said, "by not dragging my apprentice into your human business."

"You're mad at him for rescuing me?"

Oh, crap. I'd used the stone to call him to my side, which he wasn't strictly supposed to have given me in the first place. I'd known there would be consequences, but I hadn't counted on the Grim Reaper *already* being irked with me when I'd crossed that line.

"I told you," Xavier told his boss, "you can hardly blame

Rory for calling me to help her get out when the Founders had another Reaper with them."

"That's precisely why you should have stayed behind," the Grim Reaper said.

"*You* knew." Accusation lined Xavier's words. "That's why you let Maura walk away, isn't it? You knew she wasn't the rogue."

The heartbeat of silence that followed his question told me his guess was on the mark. *He knew, and he didn't tell Xavier? That's harsh.*

"You wouldn't have acted any differently if I'd told you," the Grim Reaper said dispassionately. "You forget your duties."

"I'm the one who called him to help." My hands curled into fists. "I didn't exactly have a lot of time to think of an escape plan. Not when I was trying to stop them from breaking into my mind and stealing my secrets."

The Grim Reaper remained unimpressed. "You shouldn't have ended up in that situation in the first place."

"You think I should have just left those people to die?" My heart gave a pang for Wynn, for her fellow vampires who'd perished at Carlos Verdant's hands. "Don't forget Victoire was staying in Ivory Beach. She always planned to capture me even if I hadn't gone to the other Founders' house. Xavier would have been drawn into this one way or another."

"Precisely," said a new voice. "Really, it's getting rather tiresome to watch you two continually deny the obvious."

All eyes turned to Evangeline, who stood behind the Grim Reaper, displaying no fear whatsoever at the shadows lapping around his form. Her teeth were bared, and for a terrifying instant, I wondered if the two of them were about to get into a full-blown fight here in the library.

"Deny what?" he enquired. "That your people have enticed a rogue Reaper to join their ranks?"

"Not at all," she said. "Besides, I'm here to talk to Aurora, and I'd prefer that you didn't Reap her soul first."

"Me too," I supplied. "I'd also rather you didn't get into a fight inside my home. My family members would prefer that too."

I held my breath as the Grim Reaper's shadow inched farther and farther into the lobby, while Evangeline met him step for step.

Then a sudden feathery blur came soaring over the bookshelves, aiming for the two intruders.

"Sylvester!" Aunt Adelaide came running forward, catching the owl by his tail feathers before he could crash into the Grim Reaper. "That's enough."

"Yes, it is." The Grim Reaper beckoned, and both he and Xavier vanished into the shadows.

"Hey—" I took a step back when Evangeline sauntered the rest of the way into the library. The vampires' leader watched with mild interest as Aunt Adelaide placed the disgruntled owl onto the desk.

"Begone, vampire," Sylvester hissed.

"I mean no harm," Evangeline said. "Not to you, nor to the library."

Why now? How did she always have the worst sense of timing? "What are you doing here?"

"I thought you'd want to know I identified one of the potions from the lab as one designed to prevent mind reading." She held up the bottle. "It's yours."

I blinked at her. "You *want* me to be able to block you from my mind?"

"I merely thought that this would be useful in the event that you find yourself captured again."

"Oh. Thanks." Surprised, I took the bottle from her. "Wait, was it Victoire who identified the potion? Because I'm not sure she would have been honest with you, considering she lied about everything else."

"I've dabbled in alchemy a little myself," she said. "Enough to know that in this instance, she was telling the truth."

"Ah." I picked my words carefully. "Is she in jail?"

"She is," she confirmed. "As is Carlos Verdant. I will have a satisfying time interrogating them both."

That must mean she'd paid a visit to the Grim Reaper or vice versa, where he'd handed over the vampire to her. I was sure that Carlos Verdant would rather take a vial of his own poison than submit to Evangeline, but if she'd learned from Cateline's fate, she would take steps to prevent that from happening. Either way, I would be happy never to hear anything of him again.

"Did…" I paused. "Did you intend for Victoire to lead you to Carlos Verdant? Or was that a coincidence?"

"I rather thought he'd have more sense than to stay so close to his old haunts," was her reply. "However, I cannot say I'm disappointed at the outcome."

"What about the Grim Reaper?" I asked. "I'm surprised he handed Verdant over to you without a fuss."

"Why?" She arched a neat eyebrow. "Carlos wronged me far more than he did our dear Reaper… though the same might not be said for Victoire."

I blinked. "What do you mean? Victoire said they were friends, which I know is a lie, but—"

"That," she said, "is not my tale to tell."

When she made to leave, I said, "Wait. Before you go, I just wanted to ask… did you find anything in Carlos's house? Any labs?"

"No antidotes, no." She studied my face. "Really, Aurora, have you forgotten what that library of yours was capable of? There's a reason so many of my fellow vampires want to access its secrets."

Even the library can't create something that doesn't exist.

I didn't speak the thought aloud, but I didn't hide it, either. Evangeline's searching expression remained intact. "Since when has that stopped certain family members of yours from trying to do the impossible?"

And she was gone, the door fluttering closed behind her. I stared for a moment, trying to process her words. I'd had entirely too much excitement today, and we hadn't even opened the library yet.

"What's going on?" Aunt Candace breezed into the lobby. "Don't tell me I missed more drama."

"Only a fight between the Grim Reaper and the head vampire." I dragged my gaze away from the door. "I hope he doesn't do anything too bad to Xavier for this."

Or ban us from seeing one another. He wouldn't go back on his word—I thought—but I would wait for our resident scythe-wielding grump to cool off a bit before I messaged Xavier again.

"That and she implied that we can do the impossible." Cass emerged from behind a shelf, evidently having been watching from a safe distance. "Or some of us can."

"Obviously." Aunt Candace swivelled toward me. "You didn't tell her about the corridor, did you?" Her voice gained an accusatory note.

"No," I replied. "She doesn't know specifics, and I managed to keep the other Founders from learning anything about the library at all."

"None of us would blame you if you had, Rory," Aunt Adelaide said reassuringly.

"I would," Sylvester said.

"Thanks for that," I said to the owl. "Also, was that your new ploy for attention? Picking a fight with the Grim Reaper *and* Evangeline?"

He ruffled his feathers. "*You* might not have minded them

making a mess of the lobby, but I do. I suppose you think it fits the Halloween theme."

"I forgot all about Halloween," I admitted, turning to Estelle. "Did you pick a theme? Or should we just go with something generic?"

"Sylvester, wait." Estelle held out a hand as the owl was about to take off. "Before you go off in a sulk, your dramatic swoop over the lobby would go down a treat at the Halloween party."

The owl cocked his head on one side. "You want me to terrorise the public?"

"Maybe don't go that far," she said. "But if you're going to keep destroying my balloons, you can take their place as an alternative."

"The upstairs corridor can't do that," Cass added. "You'll be the star of the show."

Sylvester puffed out his feathers in a self-important manner. "Tell me more."

"C'mon." Estelle beckoned, and to my surprise, he obliged and swooped after her across the lobby.

"I hope she manages to talk some sense into him," Aunt Adelaide said in a low voice. "The corridor isn't going anywhere, and considering what it might be capable of… You haven't been there today yet, have you, Candace?"

"Not yet," she said. "I thought I'd let Rory go next."

"What?" I tensed when both Cass and Aunt Adelaide looked at me. "I never said I was going to volunteer. I don't even know what to wish for."

"That is a lie if I ever heard one." Aunt Candace tutted. "I'll be waiting upstairs for when you change your mind."

While she strode off, Aunt Adelaide shook her head after her. "You're wise to think on your decision first, Rory. We don't know the limits on what that corridor can provide."

"Or there is no limit," Cass said. "What about that possibility?"

My dad's words came back to me, unbidden. *The most powerful spells are those which concern the magic of possibility...*

Even if no antidote currently existed, that didn't make it impossible to create one—not with alchemy or ingredients but with the pure creative magic that fuelled my family's power and pulsed through the library itself.

I straightened upright, shoulders set. "I guess there's only one way to find out."

I followed Aunt Candace's path upstairs—to the first floor, the second, then the third. As I slowed, Cass came hurrying up behind me.

"I have this." She held up the Book of Questions. "If we try both, it's bound to work for one of us."

"If we get the question right." Doubts began to seep in again. "That's the key, isn't it? Getting an antidote for a poison without a cure is far more complicated than simply finding a missing pen."

"Oh, but the principle is the same." Aunt Candace greeted us with a smile. "I knew you'd see sense, Rory."

"This had better work," I told her.

"You'll see," was her response. "Simply write your wish on the door. Don't overcomplicate matters. You'll have other chances."

"That's... strangely helpful."

"It's almost like I'm a writer or something." She laughed loudly at her own joke.

I took in a breath. If I failed, Cass could step in and try next. Or someone else could, or I could wait until tomorrow. I would have other chances. This wasn't the end.

I wouldn't let it be.

"Ready?" Cass held up the Book of Questions. "I'm going in."

"Me too." I walked past my aunt and climbed the stairs to the fourth-floor corridor.

As I reached the plain wooden door, I pulled out the pen that I used to cast my Biblio-Witch magic. No traces of the words Aunt Candace had written upon its surface remained, but a tingle of magic whispered through my fingertips when I pressed the point of the pen to the door.

Please, I thought, *grant my wish.*

"Grandma," I whispered, "or… corridor, guardian, whatever you want to be called. My heart's desire is to cure Laney of the poison. That's what I wish for."

My hand trembled as I wrote, both with nerves and with the magic tingling underneath my fingernails. When I was done, I lowered the pen. My writing glimmered on the door for a moment… then the door and the writing alike both vanished.

A small room waited on the other side, and inside was a pedestal on which sat a single feather. An inviting glimmer shone around its edges, beckoning me into the room.

I walked forward, reached for the pedestal, and picked up the lightweight object—definitely a feather.

"Is this going to wake her up?" I asked of the room, the guardian—whoever might be listening.

No reply came. Not wanting to push my luck, I crossed the threshold out of the room. At once, the door reappeared, a solid wooden frame settling into place, and without so much as a scratch on its surface.

Heart in my mouth, I walked back downstairs. Aunt Candace waited expectantly outside. "Well?"

"The room gave me this." I held up the feather. "Any ideas?"

"Yes." Cass appeared with the Book of Questions tucked under one arm and a smaller book tucked under the other. "Like I thought, I've been asking the wrong questions. Of course the library doesn't have an antidote for that particular poison, but that's not what we need."

"I don't follow." I spun the feather absently between my fingers, my gaze catching on its reddish-gold gleam. "It's pretty, but what does it do?"

"Let's find out." Cass flipped open the book she'd been carrying under her other arm, letting me glimpse the title, *Magical Monsters*. "The Room gave me this the first time I asked the question."

"What?" I lowered the feather in my hand. "You never said it'd answered you."

"I thought it was nonsense." She gave a shrug. "The book came from the Magical Creatures Division, and I've already read it backward. It's about monsters, not poisons."

"Meaning your kind of monsters?" I moved to read over her shoulder as she flipped through the pages and paused on an illustration of a large red-gold bird. "That's…"

"Phoenixes have regenerative powers," Cass said, "and if I'm not mistaken, that's a phoenix feather."

"Seriously?"

She inclined her head. "They're magically potent but impossible to find. Except, evidently, for our corridor."

"Impossible just means you aren't trying hard enough," Aunt Candace said. "What have I always told you?"

"Can it cure Laney?" There was one way to find out, I knew. "I'm going to her room."

Cass kept close behind me as I walked out of the room and downstairs. We picked up Estelle and Aunt Adelaide on the way to the living quarters, and I explained my plan, then the others peeled away when I reached Laney's room, to give us some privacy.

I entered her room, gripping the feather in one hand, suddenly overcome with uncertainty. I didn't know what I was supposed to *do* with the feather.

Cass moved behind me, impatient, pushing on my shoulder so that I stumbled over to Laney's bed. The feather began to glow a brighter gold, and instincts told me what to do next. I released the feather, which fluttered down and landed on her forehead. The glow spread across her skin, almost too bright to look at.

Then, impossibly, Laney's eyes opened.

ABOUT THE AUTHOR

Elle Adams lives in the middle of England, where she spends most of her time reading an ever-growing mountain of books, planning her next adventure, or writing. Elle's books are humorous mysteries with a paranormal twist, packed with magical mayhem.

She also writes urban and contemporary fantasy novels as Emma L. Adams.

Visit http://www.elleadamsauthor.com/ to find out more about Elle's books.

www.ingramcontent.com/pod-product-compliance
Lightning Source LLC
Chambersburg PA
CBHW061445210726
48287CB00007B/2373